"Very tense muscles you've got here, lady," Bret murmured.

Was she losing her mind? If he didn't let go of her leg immediately, she was going to melt.

"It's from chasing chimpanzees," she said with an attempt at breeziness. "Thanks, that's quite enough."

But her leg was still prisoner. His hands paused, lingering on her knee.

"Are you sure?" he asked, his voice softly teasing. She wondered if he could feel her skin pulsing to vibrant life beneath his hands, if he could read the whirling, ambivalent thoughts behind her riveted eyes.

The dreamlike setting wasn't helping at all. While tambourines jangled and the strange sound of mandolins twanged in the distance, the colors of the smoky room seemed to swirl before her eyes. If he didn't stop looking at her like that, touching her like that . . .

Lee Williams, who also writes songs and scores for musicals, lives in New York City's Greenwich Village. Although she enjoys the bright lights of the city, she's most content at home with her husband and cats, cooking up desserts of her own invention.

Dear Reader:

Summer may be ending, but this month's SECOND CHANCE AT LOVE romances will keep the fun alive. We begin with...

Anything Goes (#286) by Diana Morgan. This is the fifteenth romance—but a first for SECOND CHANCE AT LOVE—by this husband-and-wife writing team. And what a zany romp it is! Angie Carpenter, who's just been named Supermom by a national magazine, becomes so incensed by wily inventor Kyle Bennett that she vows to uphold housewives and the American way by beating Kyle's six-armed robot in a televised contest. But she doesn't reckon on falling in love with Kyle! *Anything Goes* boasts what must be one of the most original reasons for interrupting a love scene—Benny the robot arrives unexpectedly to serve lunch! Angie's mortified. You, on the other hand, may never stop laughing.

Poisoned peanut butter may sound like a "sticky" basis for a romance, but in *Sophisticated Lady* (#287) Elissa Curry adds a mouth-watering hero and a never-stuck-up heroine to create a delicious love story. The problem is that Mick Piper's being accused of poisoning his *own* peanut butter (he manufactures the stuff), and Abigail Vanderbine, who's come to interview him and ends up staying, is determined to find out who's really responsible. You'll find Elissa's magic touch in the gleefully witty repartee and oh, so sexy situations. And be sure not to miss the cameo appearance by Grace and Luke Lazurnovich from Elissa's *Lady Be Good* (#247)!

In *The Phoenix Heart* (#288) by Betsy Osborne, proper Bostonian Alyssa Courtney is sure she'll never adjust to laid-back, freaked-out California—especially once she meets gulpingly handsome cartoonist Rade Stone. Suddenly she's living in a state of constant crisis, and falling in love with a man whom her job requires she expose as an evil influence on children! Even her kids turn traitors by being on their worst behavior around Rade. Don't miss this tenderly warm romance filled with laughter and loving.

In *Fallen Angel* (#289), Carole Buck creates a powerfully emotional love story. Beautiful, vulnerable Mallory Victor is caught between two worlds: the upper-crust New England world of hero Dr. David Hitchcock, and the glittery but ultimately shallow world of rock music—where, unknown to David, she induces hysteria in teen-aged fans as rock's "bad girl," Molly V. Using both Mallory's and David's points of view to very skillful effect, Carole deeply involves us in these two characters' dilemma. Carole says *she* cried as she wrote the last thirty pages. Maybe you'd better keep some tissues handy, just in case...

Hilary Cole adds a fresh voice to romances in *The Sweetheart Trust* (#290). Here, the desirous thoughts of two mystery writers put zing into their literary collaboration. Kate Fairchild has already fallen hard for impossibly charming, delightfully unpredictable, infuriatingly witty Nick Trent. When she inherits a decrepit Victorian mansion, she seizes the opportunity to domesticate Nick in a country setting. But rural life includes unexpected—often hilarious—complications... and none of the guarantees Kate's looking for. Lots of you raved about Hilary Cole's TO HAVE AND TO HOLD romance, *My Darling Detective* (#34). You'll be even more enchanted by *The Sweetheart Trust*.

Finally, in *Dear Heart* (#291) we bring you a delightful new tale from an old favorite, Lee Williams. Why does Charly Lynn gravitate toward children and lovingly nurture the animals in the pet store she helps run? Bret Roberts doesn't have time to find out. He's too busy stealing kisses ... and trying to survive the antics of a hysterical monkey in little red pants who decides to take someone's car for a joy ride on a San Francisco hill! The fact that Bret is allergic to animals—and Charly houses innumerable dogs, cats, a rabbit, and a parakeet in her small apartment—complicates the rocky romance between this hapless couple, who are otherwise perfect for each other. Or almost ... When things get really rough, Charly writes to "Dear Mr. Heart," the local advice columnist, begging for help ... never realizing what further trouble she's getting into!

Enjoy! Warm wishes,

Ellen Edwards

Ellen Edwards, Senior Editor
SECOND CHANCE AT LOVE
The Berkley Publishing Group
200 Madison Avenue
New York, NY 10016

Second Chance at Love

DEAR
HEART

LEE WILLIAMS

A
SECOND CHANCE AT LOVE
BOOK

DEAR HEART

First edition published September 1985

First printing

"Second Chance at Love" and the butterfly emblem are trademarks be-
longing to Jove Publications, Inc.

Printed in the United States of America

Second Chance at Love books are published by
The Berkley Publishing Group
200 Madison Avenue, New York, NY 10016

Chapter

1

" 'DEAR MR. HEART: Am I an old-fashioned prude at twenty-two?' "

Trudy paused in her recitation, adjusting her bifocals and peering over the top of the newspaper to make sure Charly was listening. Charly nodded assent at the older woman, then eased a milk bottle into the eager mouth of the baby koala nestled in her lap.

" 'Last night,' " Trudy continued, " 'I had a first date with a man who wined me and dined me—then propositioned me over the chocolate mousse. Since I don't sleep with men I barely know, I turned him down. Maybe I overreacted—' "

"Charly, can you pick up on line one?"

"Char-ly? Char-ly?"

Chestnut bangs whipping past her hazel eyes as her head swiveled in both directions, Charlotte Lynn—more

1

commonly known as Charly—held up a hand to momentarily halt her senior partner's reading.

"We're still on our lunch break," she called to her assistant in the storeroom behind them. "Have 'em call back in a few minutes, Robbie, okay?"

"Char-ly? Char-ly?"

"And you, Boyd, calm down," she admonished the hungry myna bird who was querulously singing her name. "I'll get to you next." Boyd cocked his feathered head, bright eyes blinking furiously from his cage above the little alcove where the two women sat. This cozy corner in the back of the store had become their traditional lunching spot—and Trudy's reading aloud of the "Mr. Heart" column from the newspaper always accompanied their respective coffee and tea.

Trudy cleared her throat and went on. "'Maybe I overreacted—I was quite angry—but the man got huffy about it. He implied that since he'd spent a lot of money on me, I owed him something in return. At this point, I walked out. My sister insists the man's attitude is pretty typical, and I should stop being so naive. Who's right? Yours, an Irate Dater.'"

"All right, Mr. Heart," Charly murmured, wiping the koala bear's chin with her napkin. "Set the girl straight."

"'Dear Dater,'" Trudy continued. "'Stay irate!'"

"That's right," said Charly.

"'This man's attitude might be "pretty typical," but so are bad breath and wife beating. It's about time we dispense with the insulting premise that a man who spends money on a woman must be "rewarded." And if your date was crude enough to state his case in that fashion, I'd say you let him off easy. A just dessert for that turkey would be a chocolate mousse hat. Yours, Mr. Heart.'" Trudy put down the paper with a triumphant smile.

"Exactly my opinion," Charly said, nodding. "That Mr. Heart sounds almost too good to be true. You don't suppose he's really a *Ms*. Heart, do you?"

"No," Trudy scoffed. "He's just a sensitive guy."

"That's a rare breed." Sighing, Charly slowly eased the bottle out of the koala's mouth. "Full up?" she murmured as the bear closed its eyes.

"Probably not as rare as you think," Trudy said, folding her paper. "But then, how would you know, dear? You haven't exactly been—"

"Trudy," Charly interrupted, looking at her warily. "Don't start. The ink on my divorce papers is barely dry. At the moment I'm perfectly content to be leading the single life, okay?"

Trudy pursed her lips. "Perfectly content?" she queried. "What if a Mr. Heart were to walk into your life?"

Charly gave her a rueful smile. "Trudy, Mr. Heart is sensitive, understanding, warm, witty, and wise; he also sounds strong, self-assured and masculine—in print. In real life, he's probably a nasty little eunuch with a harelip."

Trudy clucked her tongue. "Charly!"

"And even if he really is as good as he sounds, he's one in a million," Charly said dryly. "Having just given four good years of my life to a man who turned out to be depressingly un-unique, I'm not in a mad rush to find another."

"Not every man is Roy Mifflin," Trudy said.

"God willing," Charly muttered.

"And all I know is, an attractive woman like you shouldn't be hiding in this little . . . cloister," she continued. "You should be out having the time of your life."

"I'm having a fine time," Charly assured her with a patient smile.

"Your mother isn't so sure about that," Trudy said.

Charly sighed. The fact that Trudy was her mother's cousin had its advantages and disadvantages. Her having hired Charly at the pet store when she moved to San

Francisco was certainly a plus, but the weekly reports
Trudy phoned back to her mom in Massachusetts were
a distinct minus. "Didn't she get my letter?" Charly asked.
"The one where I described the carefree life I was leading
on this coast?"

"Yes," Trudy said. "But it worried her that you had
enough time on your hands to write such a long letter."

Charly groaned. "You can't win," she muttered. The
phone was ringing. "I'll get it," she added quickly, glad
of the opportunity to nip another surrogate-mother lecture
in the bud.

"I'm going up the block to take a peek at the Grayson's
sale," Trudy said, as Charly rose, koala cradled in her
arms. "Want anything from the great outdoors?"

"No thanks."

"All you had for lunch was a peach yogurt," Trudy
said. "You *can't* be dieting," she added, casting a dis-
approving glance over Charly's slender form.

Charly nodded absently, picking up the telephone receiver with one hand and deftly unlocking the koala's
cage with the other. "The Sanctuary," she said into the
phone. "Can I help you?"

Trudy had her coat on and was waving good-bye. The
jingle of the shop door announced a customer's entrance,
but Charly didn't look up. She was absorbed in tucking
soft straw around the animal's fuzzy head and listening
to the man on the phone. He was the unit manager of a
film crew up from Los Angeles, and he was looking for
a lion cub.

"Well, yes, we do specialize in unusual pets, but we
don't handle lions. They're too big," she explained.

"Excuse me."

Charly turned briefly, motioning to the man on the
other side of the counter that she'd be with him as soon
as she was able. Then she quietly fastened the koala's
cage. The sated baby was already curling up into a furry

little ball of sleeping contentment.

"How about a leopard?" the unit manager was asking. "Ah, miss?"

Charly frowned, turning back around again. The man was leaning over the counter now, intent on getting her attention. Even in her annoyance, she registered his strikingly handsome features. A shock of sandy-blond hair fell over bright blue eyes. His ruggedly attractive face gleamed with a bronze tan, highlighting strong cheekbones, aquiline nose, jutting chin.

Charly cupped the receiver. "One minute," she told him, making an effort to contain her irritation. "Have you tried the zoo?" she continued into the phone.

Charly felt a little tug at the elbow of her blouse. Now, that was a bit much. She half-turned, shooting a withering look at the blond-haired man, who was leaning even farther over the counter.

He smiled apologetically. "Sorry," he began. "I was trying to—"

But Charly had already turned her back and was concentrating fully on the phone. Couldn't he wait a minute? That kind of rudeness from a customer really set her teeth on edge. "Thanks for thinking of us, though," she told the man on the phone. "And good luck."

She was just replacing the receiver when the unbelievable happened: two nimble fingers reached out and pinched her bottom!

Charly jumped around and slammed the phone down. The man was nearly climbing over the counter, his face level with her chest. Her reaction was quick and instinctive. She slapped him, hard.

The loud crack of palm against skin silenced even the ever-loquacious myna bird. The man slid back from the counter, an expression of pained shock on his face as he gingerly lifted his hand to his darkened, smarting cheek.

"Hey," he murmured. "What was that for?"

Charly crossed her arms in front of her chest. "What do you think?" she asked grimly.

"It wasn't me," the man said mildly. "That's what I was trying to tell you."

"No?" she challanged him, her eyes widening at his deceit. "I don't see anybody else who—"

Suddenly she was pinched again—even harder. Charly let out a yelp of surprise, and whirled around.

A pair of big brown eyes gazed up at her. A pair of big pink lips parted in a gargantuan grin that revealed two rows of crooked white teeth. With a maniacal cackle of glee, a hairy little chimpanzee beat a hasty retreat, darting under the counter, its big hands flapping over its face.

"Harold!" the man said sternly, reaching down to scoop up the scampering chimp. Grimacing, he lifted the chimp onto the counter, where the animal sat, cross-legged, gazing at Charly with an air of benign innocence. "I'm sorry he got away from me, but he's like that," the man said. "I was trying to get your attention when he snuck under the counter."

"I see," Charly said.

"You've got a mean right hook." He patted his reddened cheek gingerly, looking at Charly with amused respect.

"I—I'm sorry, I . . ." She faltered, feeling her own cheeks burn.

"And a very attractive blush," he added, a hint of mischief in his bright blue eyes.

"I really am sorry," she murmured.

"I haven't seen a good blush like that in some time," the man went on. "It goes with your hair."

Involuntarily, Charly put a hand up to her reddish-brown bangs, self-consciously sweeping them back from her eyes. She cleared her throat, avoiding the penetrating warmth of the man's gaze, and addressed the chimp instead. "You're a troublemaker, aren't you?" she teasingly admonished it.

The chimp gave her a look of pure chagrin and dramatically covered its eyes with its hairy hands. Charly laughed.

"He sees no evil," the man said dryly. "After he's done it, that is."

"Cute," Charly said, smiling. Her practiced eye was busily checking out the chimp: a clean, healthy coat of hair; trimmed nails; decent teeth. "Where did you get him?"

As the man didn't immediately reply, she looked up and found his vibrant blue eyes gazing at her in a way that indicated he'd been doing some checking out of his own. There was a sensuous, magnetic pull to his gaze that seemed to draw all rational thought from her brain.

"You're not from around here, are you?" he asked, his eyes holding hers captive in their soft velvet depths.

"No," she murmured, aware that he'd ignored her question, but too befuddled to pose it again.

"It shows." He pursed his lips, his gaze briefly sweeping down from her short-cropped hair to her shoulders, raking her body with a warm, intimate caress of appraisal.

"You mean the lack of tan?" she suggested, disconcerted by the openly appreciative look in his eye.

"That and the New England in your voice," he said, smiling. "Sounds fresh to my jaded Californian ears." The softness in his beautiful eyes contrasted with the strong, prominent cheekbones and thrusting chin. Charly realized she was staring and tried to stop, but it wasn't easy. What had happened to her professional demeanor? She was feeling a spidery, ticklish sensation at the base of her throat. Only when she swallowed and moved back did she realize that Harold was playing with the top button of her blouse, and the sensation was far from illusory.

"Harold!" the man said warningly.

The chimp grinned, but didn't let go—not until he'd opened the button.

"Sorry," the man said, but his eyes lingered on the pale, soft skin at the base of her throat, even as Charly demurely refastened the button. She could feel the beginnings of a deeper flush inside her.

"Where did you get him?" she asked again, keeping her eyes on the chimp. She wasn't ready to chance another glance at those vibrant blues.

"It was a friend's idea of a funny birthday present," the man said. He cleared his throat. "Monkeys don't really suit me." His smile was endearingly sheepish. "Anyway, I'd looked in here once before. I thought you people might consider taking him off my hands."

Charly looked at the man again. If he had been in before, she would have noticed him. The bronzed skin and blond hair, the muscular body framed in brown leather jacket and hip-hugging jeans . . . She would definitely have noticed him. He absolutely exuded an air of graceful yet powerful masculinity: that broad chest with its sexy little curl of hair at the open collar of his soft flannel shirt—

Good Lord, what was she thinking? Her mental circuits seemed to have gone a little fuzzy. She forced her thoughts back to business. "You mean, you want us to take him?"

"That's right," he said. There was a sensual rumble to his low voice that seemed to vibrate right through her. "I tried the zoo first, but they've got too many monkeys already. I figured you could get a decent price for him. He's in very good shape."

"Well, my partner isn't here just now," Charly began. "Trudy would have to be consulted about this."

"And what's your name?" he asked.

"Charlotte," she said.

"Charlotte?" he returned. "You're a lovely looking

lady, and that's a lovely name. But somehow I suspect . . . you're a Charly!"

And you're a flirt, she thought with a frown intended to combat his infectious smile. "You're right," she admitted guardedly. "That's what I'm called."

"I'm Bret Roberts," he returned, holding out his hand.

Charly extended her own hand after a moment's hesitation. Why shouldn't she shake his hand? Then, as his strong fingers enfolded hers, she knew her fears had been warranted. A stream of sensual electricity zinged through her at his barest touch.

Bells were ringing—but it was just the jingle of the shop door opening. Charly took her hand away, palm tingling. Harold clambered down the other side of the counter and went loping across the floor to greet the couple coming in, two students with knapsacks on their backs. One knelt down, taking the chimp's proffered hand, obviously fascinated.

"He makes friends fast," Charly noted with a smile.

"He's a devious little devil," Bret muttered, then added, quickly, as Charly looked at him: "But I'm sure your customers will love him. You could use a monkey, couldn't you?"

"Well, we did have a marmoset a few months back," she mused.

"There you go," he said expansively. "Sold him fast, I bet." He glanced behind him. "Harold'll fit right in with your pythons, parrots, ferrets, and"—he squinted at the cage to his right—"Chinese dog?"

Charly nodded. "Rare breed," she told him. "The thing is, I should really wait for Trudy—"

"What Harold needs is some warm, sympathetic care," Bret broke in. "The kind of care I saw you giving that little koala bear." Charly opened her mouth to reply, but he hurried on. "And I can see you like him already. *I* couldn't give him the attention someone like you could . . ."

His expression grew oddly perplexed as his words
trailed off. His gaze was traveling slowly over her features. Their eyes locked, and she felt an inexplicable
shiver ripple down her spine. "Say," he murmured. "We
haven't met before, have we?"

That old line! Her inner antennae vibrated, registering
a danger signal. "No," she said warily.

"Strange," he murmured. "Because when I look at
you . . ."

Charly tried to stare him down, but that was a mistake.
Her intended cool look melted in mid-trajectory.

". . . I almost feel as if . . ." Bret paused, and she
watched, riveted in spite of herself, as a web of tiny lines
softly creased the corners of his eyes. "Sorry," he said,
shaking his head with an abashed look. "I know what I
must sound like." He shrugged. "But I do get this feeling
we've already been acquainted, somehow."

She'd been about to dismiss what sounded like a standard pitch. But the disturbing this was, she was expe-
riencing a similarly strange sensation. Whenever she
looked at his face—a stranger's, but oddly familiar—
her body began humming like a tuning fork that had been
gently struck. It was most disconcerting.

"I'm sorry," she found herself saying. "But we
haven't."

"Oh, don't be sorry." Those soft smile lines sprang
up at the corners of his mouth now. "Maybe I'm only
feeling that I *want* to know you. And now that we actually
have met—what time do you get off work?"

Charly narrowed her eyes, her cynical defensiveness
returning. "Later," she said evenly.

Bret smiled. Easily, familiarly, he reached out to brush
a wisp of hair from her cheek.

"Hey, mister!"

Bret turned suddenly, and she looked behind him. The
two students were gesturing excitedly at the half-open

door. "S'cuse me," Bret muttered as he sprinted down the length of the store.

Charly watched in surprise, though she was grateful for this sudden interruption. All had been right and normal in her secure little world up until a few minutes ago. But with those luminous blue eyes staring at her, she'd suddenly felt as if she'd been blinded by slow-motion flashbulbs; and The Sanctuary's sturdy wooden floor had done an abrupt pinball-tilt beneath her feet. She craned her neck to see what was transpiring in the bright sunlight outside, but the students hovering in the doorway blocked her view.

"What's up?" Robbie asked, coming out of the back room.

"A chimpanzee on the loose." She sighed.

"I didn't know we had one," he said, confused.

"Well, I'm not sure we do, yet," she began. "But this guy—"

"Charly!"

She looked to the doorway. Bret was leaning in. "Yes?"

"Does anyone who works here own an old VW Rabbit? Dark green?"

"I do," she said. "Why?"

He was waving for her to come outside. "You're in charge," she called to Robbie as she moved quickly around the counter.

Boyd rattled his cage and sang out her name excitedly as she hurried past. Charly paused in the doorway, caught unprepared for the brisk September breezes. She was wearing only a thin silk blouse and a linen skirt.

"You didn't lock it," Bret observed, nodding toward her car.

Her VW was parked just past the entrance to the shop on Stanyan, and a monkey was sitting in the driver's seat. Harold gave her a friendly leer, pressing his fat lips up against the window.

"Well, at least I didn't leave the keys inside," she said, hugging herself in the rising wind.

"It's a good thing," Bret muttered, shaking his head as Harold gave the wheel an experimental tug. "I'll get him out."

He strode to the car and pulled at the handle. But Harold, seeing him approach, showed remarkable foresight. A hairy paw came down over the lock. Once more he lipped the window.

"Nice work," Bret said. He was about to move around the front of the car when he noticed that Charly was shivering. "Hold on a second," he said. Taking his brown leather flier's jacket off in one quick motion, he slipped it over her shoulders.

"Thank you," Charly began. "You didn't have to—"

A loud honk made them turn as one to the VW. Harold had found the horn. "Great," Bret groaned. "Next thing you know, he'll—"

The words were barely out of his mouth when the too-clever chimp released the brake. As they watched, momentarily frozen in shock, Harold began madly slapping the steering wheel, and the car began slowly sliding down the sloping asphalt.

Bret and Charly moved forward simultaneously, he cursing under his breath and she casting anxious glances behind them to see if any cars were approaching. Luckily the street was clear. And as San Franciscan hills went, this little corner near the park barely qualified.

Still, Harold was steering her car with all-too-human accuracy into the proper lane. Bret tugged at the locked door to no avail as the car continued to roll forward. "Harold!" he called through the window. "I am not amused!"

But Harold's wide grin indicated that he, at least, was thoroughly enjoying himself. Charly couldn't help smiling at the sight of the chimp, shoulders hunched over the wheel like some little old "Sunday driver" pulling into traffic with exasperating slowness.

Bret hurried around the back of the VW, which was just gathering momentum. Walking faster to keep up, Charly tried to suppress a hysterical attack of the giggles. What if he crashed? If someone had told her that morning she'd be walking alongside a chimp-driven car in the middle of Stanyan after lunch . . .

A car that had slowed behind them gave an impatient toot, and Charly waved the driver on. Bret, trotting beside the car, had gotten the passenger door open and was prepared to hop inside. "Charly!" he called. "Can you distract him?"

Charly nodded, running full tilt now. She tapped on the driver's window until Harold swiveled to look at her—and then Bret leapt into the car and lunged for the steering wheel. The VW swerved, and Charly jumped back.

Through the window she could only dimly make out Harold and Bret in what appeared to be hand-to-hand combat. The car swerved crazily again as limbs flailed in the front seat. She looked on, helpless, her heartbeat anxiously accelerating. They were heading for an intersection.

The VW abruptly veered to the right. It looked as if Bret had the upper hand. The car was out of traffic, moving to the curb, slowing . . . and then, with a squeal of brakes, shuddering to a halt, neatly parked a yard from a fire hydrant.

When she reached the VW, she found an angry Harold pummeling the head and shoulders of an equally maddened Bret. The sight of the handsome, blond-haired hunk warding off a barrage of monkey blows released her last inhibitions. Giggling in relief at the absurdity of this sight, she leaned against Harold's window.

"Funny, huh?" Bret shot her a dark look as he finally

succeeded in pinning Harold back against the driver's seat.

"I'm sorry," Charly said. "I'm just happy you're—everything's—okay."

"Everything's—oof!—dandy," he growled, teeth clenched as Harold delivered an expertly aimed kick to his solar plexus. Bret rolled the window down. "Maybe you could get a grip," Bret said. "He's—"

But Harold made a sudden bolt for freedom before she could stop him. As he jumped through the open window, past her flailing arms, and into the street, Charly felt a jolt of pure terror. There were cars coming!

Instinctively she ran after the chimp, ignoring Bret's cautionary cries behind her. Horns blared. Brakes screeched. But luckily Harold was fast and Charly's frantic arm-waving halted an oncoming motorcycle. The chimp, cheerfully oblivious, scampered up the opposite curb as Bret joined her in the middle of the street.

Charly took a shuddering breath of relief. "That little . . ."

"You little . . ." Bret glowered at her, shaking his head. "You could have gotten yourself killed."

"Well, excuse me," Charly said, bristling, despite the little tremor that shot through her at the look of concern in Bret's eyes. "I wasn't about to let him—"

Bret abruptly grabbed her hand, and before she had time to protest, he was pulling her after him. She quickly saw why.

Harold was already a blur of brown fur, disappearing, even as they ran, into the green foliage of Golden Gate Park. "Harold!" Bret called.

Her palm felt hot in his firm grasp as they slowed to a jog within the quiet shadows of tall redwoods. She was thrown completely off-balance by his brusque commandeering, and their sudden immersion into the verdant forest. When they paused at the entrance to a little clearing, she gently disengaged her tingling hand and tried to catch her breath.

"Oh great," Bret cried, looking up. Charly followed his gaze. Dimly visible amidst the emerald-green needles of a large pine, there was Harold clambering out on a branch.

"He looks right at home," she observed.

"Maybe we should just leave him there," Bret groused. As if in reply, a well-aimed pinecone spiraled toward his head. He ducked just in time. "Nice," Bret said as Charly laughed.

"Serves you right." She smiled. "Imagine, abandoning him—why, he's only a child."

"A brat, you mean," Bret corrected.

"Yes," she allowed, "but a smart one. I'm sure if we ignore him for a few minutes, he'll come scampering down."

Bret shook his head and stole a glance at his watch. Then he nodded, gave a rueful shrug, and sat down on a large tree trunk nearby. "Have a seat," he offered.

He was patting the massive stump, which did look roomy enough for two. But Charly hesitated, self-consciously glancing at her own wristwatch. "I really should be getting back," she began.

"Nonsense," he said. "How can you leave when we're having such a good time?"

Charly smiled in spite of herself at this maddening self-assurance. "I thought you'd had your fill of such . . . monkey business," she teased.

"I haven't had my fill of you," he said evenly. "Besides, I can see you've fallen in love with—"

"What!?" she exclaimed, narrowing her eyes. "I think you need some glasses, Mr. Roberts."

"—Harold," he finished, with an insouciant smile. "And the feeling seems to be mutual. You'd better wait until he comes down—or he might stay up there all day."

Charly gave her watch another glance. She could only hope Trudy was back at the shop by now. With a resigned shrug, she sat down on the trunk, trying to keep at least a foot of space between her and Bret.

Her eye was caught by the line of his profile as he looked up at the pine branches. Sunlight shining through them dappled his golden skin. He was as devastatingly handsome from this angle as he was head-on, she noted, then mentally kicked herself. What was wrong with her, anyway? She'd never before found herself so powerfully affected by a man's physical presence.

The last man to get under her skin had been Roy. And since their painful separation, she'd only tentatively played the field. The few dates she'd reluctantly accepted, mostly to appease Trudy, had only reaffirmed her suspicions about single men in California: They were just a bunch of footloose, self-absorbed hedonists—and none had interested her in the least.

Were all men hopeless, East Coast and West?

Was Bret Roberts?

Charly forced herself to look away from Bret's profile, wondering why she should think this man might actually have some depth beneath his banter. Well, there was that look in his eye, and that feeling she'd gotten when he touched her ... Charly shivered involuntarily, focusing on the dogwood and azalea still gloriously abloom in the thicket of greenery before her.

It's a purely physical phenomenon, she assured herself. A year of celibacy does have its side effects. And even if Bret Roberts was sincerely interested in something deeper than a flirtation ... she wasn't. Not anymore.

"Penny?" A husky drawl jolted her out of reverie. "Or do I need a nickel for those thoughts of yours?"

The gently quizzical smile on his face nearly brought the blush back to her cheeks. Charly feigned renewed interest in the chimp above them. "Oh, I was just thinking about Harold," she said. "Has he had his vaccinations?"

Bret paused long enough to make it clear he knew her thoughts had dwelt on something more interesting. "So far as I know," he said. "I've got his papers in my—"

"Oh!" Charly exclaimed, following his gaze. She'd forgotten she was wearing his jacket. "Here, I'll—"

But before she could even unzip the brown leather, Bret was reaching into its front left pocket. She stiffened at the intimate contact, her nostrils quivering at the scent of minty after shave as he bent over her, his eyes only inches from her own. She could feel his hand in the pocket, sliding along her midriff in a casual, unintentional caress that nonetheless sent a tremor through her body.

"Not that pocket," he said, and tried the other.

"Why don't I just—" she began, as the base of his thumb lightly grazed her breast above the pocket lining. But he was already withdrawing his hand, an innocent expression on his face, a sheaf of folded blue papers in his fist.

"Here we are," he said. "One of these is from a vet- terinarian, and another is some kind of customs form."

"Good," she said, her breath coming a bit unevenly. She leaned back. "Why don't you hold on to them for the moment? I still have to check with Trudy, you know. I mean, I'm willing to take Harold, I guess, but I can't speak for her."

"Sure," he said smoothly. "Now, the least I can do as a show of gratitude is take you out to dinner."

"Dinner?" She looked at him uncertainly. "No, that's really not a requirement."

"Requirement?" His eyes widened. "Yes, it is, actu- ally. You absolutely have to have dinner with me or the deal's off."

"Wait just a second," she said. "I might call your bluff

and you'll be stuck with Harold again."

"You're right," he murmured, frowning. Then he snapped his fingers. "I know. If you won't go out with me, I'll start bringing you a monkey a day. You wouldn't like that, would you?"

Charly smiled. "No. But where would you get them? Raid the zoo?"

"That's an idea," he said, smiling back. "So, what do you say?"

His eyes seemed to drink in her every feature as he awaited a reply. Charly considered, wavering. But even as the soft upward curve of his sensuous, full lips tempted her, she felt a cold knot of fear tighten in her stomach. She had good reasons for shunning more intimate relationships with men—damn good reasons, that she didn't enjoy thinking about.

"I don't go out with strangers," she answered carefully.

"But we're not strangers," he scoffed. "We've known each other"—he checked his watch—"a good half hour already. And look at how much fun we've had in that time."

"Fun?" she raised an eyebrow.

Those startlingly blue eyes of his lit up with a gleam that was almost devilish. "Yes, fun," he replied. "Doesn't it feel great to be sitting here on a tree stump on a gorgeous day like this? You've been cooped up in that dark little zoo too long, I can tell. The fresh air's good for you. And besides," he continued, adding a flash of white teeth to the already blinding glow of his mischievous eyes, "I'm just getting to know you better."

"Well, that's fine for you," she said, "but I don't feel I know you at all."

"Then dinner's just the thing for getting better acquainted," he said, as if such logic were unassailable. "Where would you like to go?"

Charly sighed. His arrogance was beginning to annoy her. "I'd like to go back to my store, if we can collect your chimp," she said.

"*Your* chimp," he reminded her. "He's on his way down," he added, leaning forward conspiratorially. "No, don't look." He halted her in mid-turn with a firm but gentle grip on her arm. "He thinks we don't know he's on his way over here."

The feel of Bret's fingers on her arm was electric even through the thick leather of his jacket. Charly found herself staring into those merry eyes, now only a few inches from her own. She was trapped by his gaze and his grip. Her heart drummed with excitement.

"Let go of my arm," she whispered weakly. "You don't have to—"

"But I do," he whispered back. "Don't move."

Riveted by the firefly lights she saw dancing in the soft blue depths of his eyes, Charly couldn't move away fast enough as he leaned forward, his lips alarmingly close. Her own lips were already parting, her breath slowed to a tremulous gasp, when she felt two little hands beating on her back.

She stiffened, eyes widening, started to pull away. But then the hands beat harder—pushed—and she was pitched forward into Bret's arms. His startled face flashed before her as he lost his balance, and they tumbled to the ground together in a heap.

Fortunately the thick pine needles made a natural carpet. The thud Bret's back made as it hit the ground probably wasn't as bad as it sounded, but Charly's crash-landing on his broad chest seemed to have knocked the wind out of him.

Bret lay still as Charly gazed into his eyes and noticed, with the sort of dazed removal that often accompanies disaster, that he had the thickest, softest eyelashes she'd ever seen. She also noticed, with a hot flush of arousal, that her breasts were pressed tightly against his chest and their legs were tinglingly entwined.

She cleared her throat. "Are you okay?" she asked.

"Mmm," he murmured. "Quite comfortable, actually." She could feel his husky voice reverberate through her own chest. The soft peaks of her breasts tautened as she felt his firm musculature through the thin shirt material. Charly squirmed in his arms, but he still held her tightly.

"No, don't move," he murmured, gazing into her eyes.

"Are you hurt?" she asked, concerned.

He shook his head. "Charly..." His fingers played about the hair at her neck, and his eyes seemed to draw her even closer as a delicious shiver rippled through her whole body. His full lips were only inches from her own.

"Yes?" she whispered. And then the impossible, the unbelievable happened. He lifted his head, leaning forward the few inches necessary to bring his lips to hers.

He kissed her.

And she let him.

Chapter

2

BRET'S MOUTH WAS like warm silk as it brushed hers, the softly tingling touch starting a current of fire flowing in her veins. He pursed the full, firm flesh of his lips to tease hers gently at first. Then the wispy kiss lengthened, deepened, even as she struggled feebly in his hold.

She wanted to break away. She wanted to get up. She wanted . . . him. As the hot tip of his tongue found hers, Charly's resistance began to melt. She tasted the sweetness of him, her senses overpowered by the eager, urgent thrust of his tongue, the clean, morning-dew smell of him mixing with the pine-scented ground beneath them. Then he was pulling her even closer and her body stopped resisting altogether. His tongue was eagerly exploring the moist warmth of her mouth, tracing the inside of her lips and stirring long-dormant responses of overwhelming intensity.

As her mouth melded with his, her blood rose in a primal pounding. Her skin pulsed to vibrant life beneath his touch. His fingers lightly traced the curve of her neck, and the hands she'd put up defensively against his chest relaxed. Now her palms rested lightly on his broad chest. She was filled with sensations so voluptuous she might have swooned.

She'd closed her eyes, lost in the intensity of their kiss, but opened them woozily now. His tongue, having probed her with a leisurely, wanton thoroughness, retreated, teasingly grazing the underside of her quivering upper lip. Then he brought his lips back down to capture hers once more, as she tried to focus, to think, to remember her name...

The muffled *thunk!* of a pinecone near Bret's head was what finally pulled her back to earth. She broke the kiss, blinking furiously to dispel the hypnotic force of his beautiful eyes, alight with desire. She lifted her face and took a deep, shuddering breath.

"Mmm," he murmured, looking up at her. "I had a feeling you were a passionate woman..." His voice was a husky rasp. "But I had no idea you were so aggressive!" He raised an eyebrow, the beginnings of a teasing grin tugging the corners of his mouth. "I like that in a woman."

"It wasn't me," she breathed. As she squirmed in his arms, trying to sit up, she could distinctly feel the hard evidence of his arousal against her thighs, and the flush that had already appeared in her cheeks deepened.

"No?" he murmured, his eyes widening and his arm sliding around her waist. He was evidently misinterpreting her movements as being deliberately provocative.

Charly felt a sudden blaze of anger at his insufferable conceit. "Harold pushed me!" she retorted.

"*Harold?*" As he repeated the name, they both heard the chimp's distinctive hooting laugh. Bret finally released his grip and they both attempted to sit up. The chimp was skipping in a little circle a few yards away.

Charly realized she was half-sitting in Bret's lap. And although it was a titillatingly comfortable position, it was also a dangerous one. She hurriedly stumbled to her feet—and felt a shooting stab of pain from her twisting ankle.

Bret's head whipped back at her sudden intake of breath. "What's wrong?" he said, brow creased in concern as she hopped on one foot, grimacing and holding her ankle.

"Twisted it," she told him through clenched teeth.

"Here," he said, and he half-walked, half-lifted her to the tree trunk. Charly didn't protest as he knelt, pulling off her shoe and inspecting her foot. His gentle ministrations were wonderfully soothing.

"Nothing serious," he announced after an inspection that entailed some careful probings. "See if you can walk on it."

Harold had at last come over and was clinging to Bret's leg as he helped her to her feet. Although she was able to step down, putting her full weight on the foot elicited a gasp of pain.

"Needs a little rest," Bret noted.

"Yes, that's all," she said. "Why don't I just— Hey!"

Before she had time to move away, she suddenly found herself being lifted into the air. Bret held her captive in his brawny arms, holding her aloft as if she were light as a feather. Charly had no choice but to cling to his solid frame, even as her body quaked at his nearness.

"Well, you can't walk on it," he said, his brilliant eyes twinkling. "So I'm giving you a lift. It's the least a gentleman can do."

Gentleman?

"This is ridiculous," she began. "You don't have to—"

"It's a pleasure," he interrupted, smiling. "We're getting so much closer, and in such record time."

Charly opened her mouth, but immediately rejected the stream of expletives that came to mind as too unlady-like. She'd lost enough of her dignity as it was. And they were already walking down the path through the pines, Bret bearing her weight with ease. Still mortified by her enthusiastic response to his kiss—and smarting from his insinuation that it was something she'd actually engineered—she tried to make herself comfortable.

Comfortable, however, was not the word for the way she felt in his arms as they followed the path toward a clearing. It was hard enough to be captive, yet feel her palm tingle as she grasped his tanned neck and felt his soft blond hair tickle her wrist. And it was even harder not to squirm with unwanted sensual arousal at the feel of his arms cushioning her as they walked. But emerging out of the woods and into a tourist-packed Japanese tea garden in the arms of Bret Roberts, a chimpanzee at their side, was worst of all.

"Good God!" she wailed. "Half of San Francisco's going to see this!"

A bevy of tourists were sipping tea and eating little cookies in an authentic Japanese-style pagoda that over-looked sculpted gardens and ponds filled with giant gold-fish. Some had already noticed the odd trio coming out of the woods and into the bright sunlight. Bret chuckled good-naturedly at the cries of excitement their appearance elicited. Cameras were quickly unslung from countless necks. People of all ages and nationalities abandoned their tea to get a closer view. Bret obliged them by car-rying her slowly around the edge of the garden.

"I can't look," Charly muttered, turning her crimson face into Bret's neck as the first camera clicked. But that was a mistake she realized when her lips tasted the salty-sweet skin at the base of his throat and her heart began pounding all the louder.

"They probably think we're Tarzan and Jane," he said. "Well, it's too bad I have to get back to my office soon; otherwise we could stop in for a cup of tea."

Harold, being a natural ham, was grinning broadly, climbing halfway up Bret's leg and leaning back, big lips pursed, in an absurd parody of a pin-up's pose as cameras clicked, children laughed, and adults gawked. Charly didn't think she could bear another minute of it.

"Put me down," she pleaded. "Do you think I'd go in there and sip tea after being made the laughingstock of Golden Gate Park?"

Bret shrugged. "Okay, Charly," he said. With a last wave at the group of onlookers gathered at the edge of the tea-house garden, he carried her back toward the clearing they'd come out in and slowly lowered her to the ground. But he kept her close to him, so that every inch of her soft curves rubbed slowly against his harder lines en route. And just as her feet were touching earth, he pulled her tightly up against him, his mouth once more swooping down to capture hers.

Again she began to struggle, started to squirm from his grasp, and then surrendered helplessly to the warm pulse of unbridled desire that filled her being from the inside out. The man knew how to kiss. As he wrapped both arms around her, crushing her now pliant body to his, his moist, sensuous lips claimed hers. Resistance was useless. Time stopped and the world spun. She reveled in the urgent thrusts of his eager tongue, breathlessly responding with a fervor that dimly shocked her. She was lost, awash on waves of sensuous sensation . . .

. . . until the sound of still another camera click and a child's giggle brought her abruptly to her senses. Charly broke from Bret's grasp, her face reddening as she beheld two little girls in school uniforms snapping their photo from a few yards away. Harold was lolling around in the grass at their feet, miming loose-lipped kisses at the wide-eyed children.

"Did you have to do that?" Charly fumed. She pushed Bret away from her with an involuntary wince as her still-weak ankle throbbed with the effort.

"I'm sorry," Bret said quickly, a look of genuine contrition on his face. "I couldn't help myself, really. It's those lips of yours," he said earnestly. "They're completely irresistible. And your eyes, of course—they seem to contain so many different colors, and they glitter like jade when you're being defensive."

Charly stared at him, swallowing hard as his deep mesmerizing voice threatened to evaporate that very defensiveness. His sky-blue eyes still glowed with small pinpoints of smoldering desire. Even as she drew away, her thoughts went hazy as his eyes continued to hold hers.

"But they aren't green, really," Bret continued. "They're a tawny, earthy color, like a dew-soaked field in a summer meadow."

His hand was still grasping hers, and he squeezed it gently. Charly flinched, commanding her palm to slide from his, though it remained a stubbornly willing prisoner. Bret felt her stiffen and let it go, a slight smile hovering at the edges of his sensual lips.

"Oh, I know I'm not a poet," he said. "But the writer in me is looking for the proper words to capture that beautiful light in your eyes." His smile widened. "You think I'm handing you a line."

"That's right," she said, though a part of her had just been adrift, spellbound and believing, in thrall. She winced again as she took another step back, her ankle giving way.

"Here, lean on me," Bret offered quickly, his brow creasing with concern. Charly didn't have much choice. Tentatively she took hold of his shoulder. "Harold!" he called, then turned back to her. "Let's get you home."

The chimp bounded over, obedient for once, and Bret grabbed its hand. With a supporting arm around Charly, he turned and led her toward the path leading back into the woods. Charly adjusted her weight, both thankful for his help and vaguely resentful of it.

The sudden silence between them resounded with unspoken thoughts. She didn't know which was more discomforting—her throbbing ankle or the nearness of him. Even if he had just spun her some kind of practiced line, Bret's physical magnetism was undeniably potent. She mentally rummaged for an innocuous conversational gambit to get her mind off the feelings he'd stirred up inside her.

"So you're a writer?" she ventured.

"Of a sort," he said. "I'm a journalist/newspaperman/ reporter/editor."

"Is that all?" she joked, relieved that he'd allowed her to change the subject.

"Keeps me busy," he said. "How about you? Do you work in that place full-time?"

Charly nodded. "My pets are my work," she said.

"I tend to be more interested in people," he commented.

"You don't like animals?"

"A select few. I'm allergic to cats. And I might be developing an aversion to apes," he added with a wry glance at Harold.

"Who do you write for?" Charly asked.

"Three or four magazines. I'm an associate editor at *Omnibus* and a contributing editor at *S.F.* Plus, I write for a couple of papers and I freelance for the *Sporting News.*"

Charly nodded absently. Her main concern was getting out of the park and back to the safety of The Sanctuary without any more embarrassing adventures. And if she could simply concentrate on this harmless conversation and watch her footing carefully, she thought she might be able to ignore the subtle vibrating of her body as it grazed his.

"But you still haven't answered my most important questions," Bret said.

"Which are?"

"What time you get off work and where you'd like to eat dinner," he said smoothly. "Although if that ankle of yours swells up, we might have to resort to my home cooking."

Charly paused in mid-stride, staring up at Bret's innocent expression. "Wait a second," she said evenly. "Who said we were having dinner?"

He frowned in mock-concentration. "Someone around here, I could swear it . . . Harold? Was that you?"

The chimp ignored him, inspecting a trail of purple wisteria at the side of the path. Charly shook her head. "Bret, I'm not really interested," she said in her most detached manner. But detachment was difficult, with her hand still on his shoulder for support.

"Funny," he said. "I'm getting some very mixed signals from you."

"I'm not sending out any signals," she said, while a little voice inside informed her that she didn't sound very convincing.

"I think you are," he said breezily. "Some very receptive—and deliciously provocative—yes's, with some equally disturbing no's."

"I'd listen to the no's if I were you," she said pleasantly, trying not to dwell on the alarming way she'd lost all control when he'd kissed her. She was glad to see they were approaching the street where they'd first entered the park.

"But the yes's are so much more interesting," he said. "Walk for me, will you, Charly?" He was indicating the edge of the sidewalk. She took a tentative step forward, lost her balance, and tottered. Bret quickly grabbed her arm. "That was a hobble," he observed. "I think you should take a little rest."

"I'm fine," she protested, more determined than ever to get back to the store and away from him. But Bret led her gently, firmly, over to a bus-stop bench just outside the park.

"Sit," he commanded.

Charly gave an exasperated sigh and sat, glaring up at him. "You know, I'm a working woman," she began. "Trudy's probably wondering—"

"Excuse me," Bret broke in suddenly, looking past her. Swiveling to see what had caught his attention, Charly spotted a shabby-looking white-bearded old man approaching them. He had on baggy pants and an un-tucked shirt. The flimsiest of sandals flapped from his gnarled feet.

"Oh, I think he's harmless," Charly began, as Bret moved forward, apparently to steer the derelict to another bench.

"He's a friend of mine," Bret told her.

She stared, incredulous, as he hailed the old man with a friendly wave. The man looked up, smiling toothlessly, and pumped Bret's hand. As she watched, they talked, and the man pulled a bunch of white pamphlets from a big canvas satchel draped over his shoulder. Bret took a thick handful and then reached into his own pocket. He paid the man—amply, it seemed to her, from the wad of bills she glimpsed—before returning to Charly's side.

"That's Ernie, the poet laureate of Golden Gate Park," Bret said, smiling. "I take it you're not familiar with his work."

"No," Charly said, looking at the pamphlets Bret brandished in front of her.

"Ernie's a walking piece of San Francisco history," Bret explained. "Kerouac, Ginsberg, Burroughs—he knew them all. He was around for the whole Beat scene, and more. He writes haiku poems on these sheets of paper—hand-printed—and hawks them on the street. Not the easiest way to make a living, so I try to help him out when I can."

"So you're a patron of the arts," Charly said. Her tone was facetious, but she was actually touched that Bret would take an interest in someone she'd have automatically dismissed as a bum.

"Hardly," Bret scoffed. "But I am writing him up for a series of articles I'm doing on San Francisco celebrities. Local ones," he added, at Charly's puzzled look. "People who've made this city the incredible mixed bag it is."

He was stuffing the pamphlets into one of the pockets of his flier jacket—which she was still wearing!—as he spoke. Charly stiffened again at the casually intimate contact, but affected nonchalance. "You'd better get Harold," she cationed. "He looks ready to bolt again."

Bret turned and nodded. The chimp was perched on the curb a few yards away, eyeing a pair of bicycling teenagers emerging from the park. They had caught sight of him and were pointing, fascinated. Harold, enjoying the attention, was already getting up to greet his new fans. Bret left Charly to fetch him.

Charly turned back to inspect her foot, and found herself looking into the clear and curious blue eyes of a little girl strapped in a stroller by the bench. She had pursed pink lips and a button nose in a round, porcelain-shiny face. Seeing Charly, she smiled, her tiny hands waving in the air.

Charly felt her heart stop, melt; felt time suspend as the child, who couldn't have been even two years old, continued to smile and stare at her. Charly swallowed, a yearning ache blossoming within her as the girl's young mother, now sitting on the bench beside her, pulled the stroller out of Charly's way, flashing an apologetic smile.

Charly smiled back, wanly, and turned again to gaze blankly in the direction Bret had gone. There it was again. It was a feeling she had tried hard to suppress. An echo of her own loss was resonating inside of her, the inner ache deepening with painful memories that just wouldn't go away.

"Charly?"

Startled, she looked up. She'd been staring through Bret as if he wasn't there. Now he knelt down to study her face with a puzzled frown. "Anybody home?" He squinted. "Foot hurting you?"

"No," she said quickly, exhaling a deep breath. She rose, stepped forward awkwardly, and faltered. Bret's hand was instantly at her elbow.

"Lady, you're almost completely disabled," he said with a wry smile. "Look, at this rate we'll never get across Stanyan without holding up traffic, so—"

"Don't you dare!"

But she was too late. Airborne once again, Charly settled, against her will, into the cradle of Bret's powerful arms. Her heart beat furiously as he carried her from the bench.

"If you're trying to impress me with your strength," she murmured, "it's not working."

"No, I just like holding you," he said.

Charly bit her lower lip and watched the approaching sidewalk as they crossed in front of a line of cars, people leaning out of their windows for a better look at Harold. Charly closed her eyes, unconsciously burying her head in the crook of Bret's shoulder, resigned to being a local spectacle for another few minutes.

Realizing she must seem a much-too-willing captive in Bret's arms, she straightened up. "You can put me down, now," she instructed as he stepped up on the curb.

"Your store's only a block or so from here," he said. "Don't be silly."

"Bret," she said, exasperated. "I can walk—"

"Hobble," he corrected.

"—there perfectly well. So would you please put me down."

"You need more padding," he mused, oblivious. "That's what you need: good food to put some meat on your bones, good fresh air to put some healthy red in your cheeks. Don't get me wrong," he corrected himself hurriedly, as she let out a frustrated moan. "I'm not criticizing your figure. It's quite . . . ah, something." He cleared his throat. "But I can tell you don't weigh enough for a woman of your height."

"Bret!" she cried. "I didn't ask for your opinions. All I'm asking is that you let me get to my store on my own two feet, instead of—"

"Lovely feet," he said calmly. "So we wouldn't want to ruin one of them. Anyway, we're almost there."

He was right, and there wasn't much she could do, except listen to the sound of her heart thundering in her ears as they approached The Sanctuary's front door.

And would he put her down before they walked inside? Of course not. He maneuvered the door open with her still in his arms, pushing Harold in ahead of them. Charly had to admit that the look on Trudy's face was almost worth the acute embarrassment of their dramatic entrance.

The older woman's owllike eyes bulged behind her bifocals, and her jaw literally dropped. Gazing up at the tall blond stranger with Charly in his arms and a chimpanzee at his side, Trudy froze. Then, recovering some vestige of composure, she came out from behind the counter and met them in the aisle.

"Who's your friend?" she asked Charly, eyes moving from chimp to man in a quick assessment.

"You must be Trudy," Bret said, all hearty friendliness. "I'm Bret Roberts. Charly's sprained her ankle. Got a place to soak it?"

I'll tell *you* where to soak it, Charly nearly muttered, but she merely gave Trudy a helpless look.

Trudy smiled. Suddenly the older woman seemed supremely happy. "Of course," she said cordially. "Come into the back."

"Trudy!" Charly wailed. "He doesn't have to—"

"We bathe the animals in here," Trudy continued to Bret, totally ignoring Charly. "Now if you'll just set her down on this table, I'll bring a portable tub over."

"Trudy," Charly said again, as Bret carried her through the swinging door. Robbie, who'd been treating a rash on their gerbil family, looked up, registered the visitors' entrance, and returned to his job.

"Yes, dear?"

"It's Harold you should be looking at. I'm fine, really. He's the one we're supposed to be taking care of. Do we have a big enough cage?"

Trudy paused in the act of wheeling the mini-tub toward her. As Bret finally lowered Charly onto a desktop, she peered up at him, then gazed myopically at Charly, confused. "We don't have any *that* big," she reflected, then addressed Bret. "Didn't you say your name was Bret?"

"Trudy," Charly said tersely. "Harold is the chimp."

"Chimp? Oh!" She looked from Bret to the monkey, smiling. "Hiya, short, dark, and handsome."

Harold gave her his most disarming grin. "Bret wants to donate Harold to us," Charly informed her. "What do you think?"

"Certainly," Trudy said, absently patting the chimp's head. "Now, you just turn this nozzle here," she instructed Bret. "Wait till the water's hot enough, and then you can put the stopper in."

Charly sighed. It was useless to protest, when Bret was already untying her shoelace and Trudy was so obviously taken with the handsome stranger that she could barely spare a glance for poor Harold. Charly was beginning to feel a bit invisible herself.

"I can do it," she told Bret quickly, as he reached for her sock.

"How did you happen to meet Charly?" Trudy asked, smiling at Bret.

"He came into the store," Charly told her. "With his monkey. This monkey, here," she said meaningfully. "Whom you might have Robbie look over as soon as he's done with the gerbils."

Bret, having tested the water, was patiently filling the little tub. "Let's see it," he said to Charly.

Charly finished rolling up her pants leg and extended the foot. It did look a bit swollen. As she gingerly lowered it toward the half-full tub, Bret and Trudy began a debate on the relative merits of the hot-water versus the ice-cube methods. By the time they'd agreed on a good soak first, followed by an ice pack, she felt ready to scream. Trudy was treating Bret the way a surrogate mother would treat a prospective son-in-law; and both of them were ignoring Charly—and the restless chimp scampering around the room, looking for trouble.

"Robbie," Charly called, over Bret and Trudy's medical powwow. "Grab that chimp, will you? We need to check out his health. Here," she said, rummaging through the pockets of Bret's flier jacket and handing the younger man the folded papers. "His certificates."

Robbie nodded, looked them over, then cleared his throat, a confused expression on his face. "'My love-worn soul of silence sings,'" he read. "'Rose petals of the Haight Street morning . . .?'"

"Wrong papers," Charly muttered, reddening, and took the pile of Ernie's poems from the bewildered assistant. She retrieved the certificates from Bret's other pocket and handed them over.

"Too hot?" Bret was asking, indicating the tub of water.

"No," Charly told him. "I'm perfectly fine now. Thank you for all your well-meaning but unneccessary attention and—"

"Charly," Trudy chided, clucking her tongue.

"—and I'd appreciate it if you'd just let me sit here quietly and relax. That's what I'd like," she said in a cheerful tone that had an edge of menace. Bret was smiling, enjoyment of the entire ridiculous situation shining in his bright blue eyes.

"Certainly," he said. "Give it about five minutes, and then we'll apply the ice."

"We won't do anything," she said pointedly. "Thank you for your help. Thank you for your chimp. Now, please, Bret"—she gave him an imploring look—"let me take care of myself. Okay?"

Bret's lips twitched mischievously. "Okay, Charly," he said. "But I'll be back. Later."

Charly shook her head. "No, that's quite all right," she said. "There's absolutely no need for you to come back."

"Oh yes there is," Bret said. He seemed about to say something else, but apparently thought better of it. Instead, he merely smiled and extended his hand. Charly swallowed and put out her own hand. Bret held it a beat too long, long enough to cause little shivers of arousal to course from her captive palm to the rest of her body. Then he lifted the hand to his lips and kissed it lightly, lowered it, and at last let go.

Charly could hear a soft, dreamy sigh escape Trudy's lips. She herself was momentarily dazed by this chivalrously sensual move, but she did her best to appear blasé, putting her hand back in her lap as if it weren't tingling all over and throbbing with the gentle imprint of his warm lips.

"I'll see you later," Bret said casually, and turned toward the door.

A sudden commotion from Robbie's corner made him pause. Harold, whimpering and flailing in the assistant's grip, was obviously upset by his former master's departure. Bret turned back and quickly strode over to the chimp, giving his head a friendly pat.

"So long, fella," he said. Harold reached up and gave Bret's nose an affectionate tweak. Charly couldn't suppress a smile. But she hurriedly tried to mask it as Bret turned toward her again, his eyes caressing her face with the intensity of smoldering searchlights.

"I'll show you out," Trudy said. She held the swinging door open for Bret, giving him a radiant smile.

"Au revoir," Bret murmured to Charly. Once his back was turned, Trudy shot Charly a withering look of incredulity, a look that asked: How could you possibly be sending the good Lord's gift to womanhood away like this?

Charly frowned as the doors swung shut. She leaned over to inspect her foot, and a few stray pine needles fell from her hair. Pine needles . . .

She could hear the tinkling of the bell and the sound of the shop door shutting behind him. It was a good thing he'd already left. Because as her memory lingered over that first kiss in the park, Charly's face turned a bright shade of red. Had he seen it, that rosy blush would undoubtedly have pleased him no end.

Charly bit her lip. She never should have let the conceited lug take advantage of her like that. And what made him so certain she had any desire to see him again? "See you later," he'd said, and *"au revoir."* Fat chance, she told him silently, shoving her hands deep in the pockets of—

—his jacket.

"Oh, no," Charly groaned, looking down in chagrin. That's what he'd been about to tell her, wasn't it? But he hadn't—purposely—that devious . . .

"Excuse me?" Robbie was staring at her, not sure he'd really heard the sudden curse word Charly hissed between clenched teeth.

"Nothing," Charly sighed. "I was just thinking up a name for a particularly weasellike mammal!"

Chapter

3

"BRET ROBERTS? LET me check. Hold on a second, will you?"

Charly held on, impatiently pacing back and forth behind the counter. She'd started out with a call to *Omnibus* magazine, where she'd apparently just missed Bret. They'd transferred her to another magazine, and the person there had given her yet another number. Everyone seemed to know Bret, to think he *might* be on the premises but might not be. And everyone was glad to pass her along to someone else. If this, her fourth call, was unsuccessful, Charly would consider donating his jacket to the Salvation Army.

"He's just come in," a pleasant voice announced. "Who should I say is calling?"

Charly exhaled a deep breath. "Charlotte Lynn," she said, feeling just a bit apprehensive. A click on the line indicated she was being transferred.

"Charlotte?" The teasing lilt of his husky voice conjured him up vividly in her mind. "Now, is that a city in Virginia or the most beautiful woman in San Francisco?"

"Neither," Charly said dryly. "You forgot your coat."

Bret chuckled. "I was going to mention that," he said breezily, "but you seemed in such a hurry to get rid of me."

"Where would you like me to drop it off? I mean, at which of your many places of work?"

"It looked very good on you," he mused, ignoring her businesslike tone. "You should have something like that to keep you warm . . . or someone."

"I'd like to return it to you," she said evenly, trying to ignore the way the hairs on the back of her neck kept standing up each time his throaty voice caressed her ear. "As soon as possible. So if you'd just tell me where—"

"Hard to say," he replied. "Let's see. Editorial meeting at *S.F.*, photos to select over at the *Herald* . . . I tell you what," he said with sudden decisiveness. "Can this wait until dinnertime?"

"I suppose," she said warily. "But I'm not interested in dinner, Bret."

"No problem," he said. "But you see, I'm running late on account of some time off I took for a chimp chase and so forth. Caught hell from my editor here, and I've got about a thousand things—"

"Sorry I inconvenienced you," she said. "But nobody *asked* you to spend time—"

"It was more fun than I've had in a long time," he said softly, and she could just see his laughing blue eyes sparkling as he spoke. "I don't have any regrets, Charly. I'm just explaining why I won't be able to hook up with you until later. How does seventy forty-five sound?"

"I guess it's okay," she said, doubtfully. "But where?"

"I'll be between appointments," he said. "Meet me at 917 O'Farrell Street, between Taylor and Jones."

Charly grabbed a pencil from the register shelf and quickly jotted down the address. "What magazine is that?"

"It isn't," he said. "But I'll be there. Seven forty-five. All right?"

"Okay," she said. "I'll just run in and give you the jacket."

"Sure," he said breezily. "I can't wait to see you. And I look forward to seeing how fast you can run on that beat-up ankle of yours."

"Very funny," Charly snapped, and hung up.

"Well?" said Trudy.

Her senior partner had, of course, been eavesdropping, hovering by the nearby cages throughout Charly's conversation. "I'm dropping off the jacket," Charly told her. "As you may have heard."

"Good for you, dear," Trudy said. "It's about time you had a date."

"It's not a date," Charly said. "I'm just running in and out."

"What have you got against dating, anyway?" Trudy queried.

"After the three turkeys you set me up with, how can you ask?" Charly replied.

"Well, just because none of them was quite right for you . . ."

"And neither is Bret Roberts," Charly said. "He's going to get his jacket back, and that'll be the end of it."

"What a shame," Trudy murmured.

Charly gave her a scathing look. "Maybe *you'd* like to have dinner with him," she said.

The address Bret had given her was near Union Square, a touristy part of San Francisco's business district. Charly walked up the block once and then back again in the cool evening air before she realized that the place she was looking for was a Moroccan restaurant.

She stood contemplating the elegant entrance, with its gaily painted Moorish archway. What was Bret Roberts doing in there, researching an article on foreign foods of the downtown area? Not likely. Charly stepped through the doorway, a disgruntled frown clouding her face.

She was greeted by a smiling man in business suit and red fez with black tassel dangling. When she asked, he checked his book. Yes, there was a Mr. Roberts within; and yes, he was expecting her.

The maitre d' guided her through another elaborately painted archway, to a waiter dressed in traditional Arabian garb. She followed him, her eye drinking in every colorful detail of the exotic surroundings: intricate tilework, splashing fountains of bright blue water; cut-brass lamps that reflected rose and copper light on the hand-painted gold-leaf ceiling; straw baskets lay strewn about the bases of columns, as if left there after a Moroccan market delivery.

Through another archway she glimpsed a band of musicians in red-and-gold costumes, and the flash of jewels and bare limbs that intimated native dancers. Looking around at the well-to-do patrons seated at tables, Charly felt a bit self-conscious. After work she'd purposely changed into a pair of baggy pants, a loose man-tailored shirt, and her favorite—albeit frayed—cardigan sweater. This outfit was intended to subtly sabatoge any hint of seductive femininity in her appearance. She didn't want Bret thinking she'd dressed up to see him.

She'd gone light on her makeup as well. The long lashes over hazel-green eyes didn't need any touching up. Hazel, she repeated mentally—not dewy grass, or whatever malarky he'd been spouting. Charly cast a nervous glance over the waiter's shoulder.

A pair of teasing, gleaming eyes in a tanned, handsome face caught hers. Bret was seated in a private alcove richly carpeted with Berber rugs. The waiter wordlessly seated her opposite him on a goatskin ottoman that was strewn with velvet pillows.

"There you are," Bret said, smiling.

"Here's your jacket," she said quickly, setting it down on the carved brass table. Another smiling waiter hovering close by offered her a towel soaked in warm water in a clay bowl. Charly looked up at him uncertainly.

"It's to wash your hands," Bret said.

"But I'm not staying," Charly declared.

"Of course you are," he scoffed. "You haven't eaten yet, have you?"

"Well, I . . ." She paused, unable to ignore the delicious aromas wafting toward her from nearby tables. She'd already caught sight of a number of mouth-watering delicacies artfully arranged on the plates she'd passed. "I'm not hungry," she lied. "And I'd planned on, ah . . ."

"Eat at home? Alone?" Bret shook his head with a sorrowful expression. "That's no fun," he murmured.

"Really, Bret, I'm not hungry. I can't stay for dinner." But of course her traitorous stomach chose that moment to growl. Bret smiled. Charly bit her lip.

"Maybe just a little snack," he suggested. "It's on me."

"I'm being coerced." she sighed.

Bret chuckled. "Good. Now wash your hands."

Shaking her head, Charly at last accepted the finger bowl and towel from the patient waiter. The water was warm and smelt faintly of roses. Next, she was proffered another, larger towel.

"That's your napkin," Bret explained. "Hold onto it— you'll need it! We're going to be doing most of our eating without silverware."

"With our hands?" The waiter was nodding with an amiable smile, as his assistants set baskets bearing small hot loaves of bread on the table before her.

"We share everything," Bret told her. "There are a number of courses that you can scoop up with hunks of bread: the salad, the couscous . . . And there'll be platters of chicken and lamb that you're supposed to eat with your fingers. You don't mind, do you?"

"I thought I was only having a snack," she said.

"Don't worry, you can just pick." Bret smiled.

"It does sound like fun," Charly admitted, glancing around her again. There was a feast steaming on another table nearby, and even now their waiter was bringing soup, apparently the standard first course here. Bret began to confer with him and Charly sat back, grudgingly reconciled to at least enjoying some interesting food.

She might have known that a man as persistent as Bret would trick her into a full-fledged dinner date. Looking him over with narrowed eyes, Charly tried to imagine what would occur during the hour to come. Would he be like Daniel, the non-stop braggart she'd gone out with a month ago? That had been exhausting. Then there was Stuart, who, though less blatantly boastful, had talked on interminably about his work. Most men she knew were wont to do just that. Bret Roberts probably had an ego to match Daniel's or Stuart's, if not one that would surpass both. Charly mentally steeled herself for an onslaught of macho monologue.

"So, Charly Lynn," Bret said, settling back against the pillows. "What brings you west of the Rockies anyway? This town is made up of equal parts natives and expatriates, but everybody's got a good reason for being here. What's yours?"

Charly stared at him, caught off guard. "Well, Trudy offered me a job," she said carefully. "She's my mother's cousin," she added, as he continued to look at her expectantly. "I heard she needed help with The Sanctuary, and I was ready for a change of pace, so I—"

"A change of pace from what?" he asked.

Charly blinked. "From . . . Boston," she said, then paused. That should be enough, she reflected. Here's where he would begin explaining why San Francisco was the best city in the country, and why he was doing what he did in it as well as he did. That had been Daniel's tack.

"What's wrong with Boston?" he queried. "Are the animals too conservative there?"

Charly smiled despite herself. "Well, no," she said. "But I liked the idea of a fresh start."

"You should start on that soup," he said. "But then you have to stop being so mysterious. What did you leave behind, anyway—a prison record?"

Charly paused in the act of lifting a savory spoonful of soup to her mouth. "No," she murmured, and tried to hide the blush she felt seeping into her cheeks. She hadn't expected Bret to be quite so inquisitive.

"Maybe you should start from the beginning," he suggested, after they'd both sipped their soup in silence for a moment.

"Beginning of what?"

"Your story, of course," he said.

Charly looked up from her soup, sniffing involuntarily as the spicy mixture cleared her sinuses. "My story?" she echoed, bemused.

"I'm sure you've got one," Bret said, a smile hovering around the edges of his sensual lips. "Journalist's instinct. Beautiful woman starts new life on distant coast selling Chinese dogs and iguanas . . . How's the soup? Like it?"

"Yes," she said, feeling her own features relax in a smile she hadn't intended. "Wouldn't you rather talk about your own work? I'm sure it's more interesting than mine."

"Nonsense," he said. "Now begin. You were born at an early age . . ."

Charly laughed. "I'd rather eat my soup," she protested.

Bret nodded. "I love your laugh," he said simply. "I think I'm going to make hearing it again a top priority."

Charly could hear her own heartbeat abnormally loud in her ears. She looked away, trying to concentrate on the bowl of soup. But her body was vibrating oddly again, and as her eyes moved from his she couldn't help but notice that sexy curl of chest hair at the opened button of his shirt. *Sip!* she commanded herself.

"You weren't born in Boston, though," he prodded.

"No," she admitted, and dabbed at her lips with her napkin. This curiosity—this interest—wasn't what she'd expected from a man like Bret.

As she continued sketching the outlines of her moving and settling in, and talking about the business at the store, she had the feeling Bret was listening more to what she'd left out than what she was filling in. He didn't press her for more personal details, though, and seemed content to discuss the store and her work there.

By the time she'd talked and munched her way through a delicious pastry course made up of shredded meat, almonds and spices, and was ready for the platter of chicken, olives, and lemons, and lamb with honey, Bret's low-key, leisurely questioning had set her entirely at ease. She was even—almost—getting used to the way his glimmering blue eyes studied her face, sometimes seeming to peer right into the depths of her very being. The heady mixture of wine and rich food, with all its exotic trappings, was lulling her into a surprising state of conviviality.

"How did you get so involved with animals?" he asked, a piece of lamb poised between thumb and forefinger. He made the act of eating with one's fingers seem entirely natural, even gentlemanly. "Did you grow up with them?"

Charly patted her lips with her napkin. "In a way. I

grew up on a sort of mini-farm in Peeksville. It's a small town near Marblehead in Massachusetts. We had some chickens, dogs, cats...no commercial cows or anything, though. My father was a carpenter, but he also acted as a lay vet when any of the animals took sick. People would bring their pets over sometimes."

Charly warmed to the task of recounting that rosy part of her past. Once the mother of a newborn sheep from a neighboring farm had died, and her dad had brought the lamb into the house. He'd let her hold it in her arms by the fireplace, all swathed in blankets. She remembered the look in its open, staring eyes, a look she'd imagined was full of trust and love. When the lamb laid its little woolly head in her lap and slept, she'd nearly cried.

Then there was the flock of ducks that had followed her in single file around the yard one whole summer. Motherless as well, they'd blindly adopted her as their leader. Her father used to roar with laughter at the sight of Charly, pony tailed and in overalls, walking down the path out back with five little white ducklings in a sober, soldierly column at her heels.

"I'd like to have seen that," Bret chuckled. "You were probably the definition of *cute* in overalls."

"Ugly as a duckling," she demurred.

"Hard to believe," he protested softly, his eyes holding hers. "So, you inherited your father's way with animals."

"I didn't have a knack for carpentry," she said. "So something had to rub off."

Bret nodded, offering her an olive. Charly took it from him, their slippery fingertips touching briefly. She shivered involuntarily, then watched, mesmerized, as he licked the end of one finger. The waiter rustled at her side. She glanced over, eyebrows raised in comic horror at the appearance of yet another platter. "More?"

"Couscous with vegetables," Bret informed her. "We'll put some weight on you, yet."

Charly shook her head, breaking off the smallest piece of bread possible. "Just a taste," she announced, and Bret smiled. It occurred to her that this was a rare date indeed. He couldn't have been more unlike Daniel. Ironically, Bret's reticence about his own life was making her genuinely curious about him.

"Did you grow up here?" she asked.

Bret shook his head. "Farther south, below Los Angeles," he said. "In Laguna Beach."

"Any animals?" She grinned.

Bret shook his head. "Just a golden retriever."

"And what sort of interests did you inherit from *your* father?" Oddly, her lighthearted question seemed to give Bret pause. His expression sobered, and the shrug he gave was eloquently embittered.

"An interest in living my life differently from his," he said, his tone indicating that he'd said all he cared to say on that subject. Then he smiled, obviously aware that he'd been abrupt. "We don't get along too well," he added. "My father was never much of a family man. His job always came first."

Charly said nothing, merely waited to see if he'd continue. She'd always taken her own family's closeness for granted. Now she felt a twinge of gratitude that the Lynns had always been—and still were—a close-knit clan, even if they were living at opposite ends of the country.

"Tell you what," Bret said, his tone once more bantering and light. "Let's stick to you tonight." His former cheerfulness seemed undampened. "You still haven't told me all I'd like to know."

"But I've been talking too much," she protested. "Aren't you bored yet?"

"Impossible," he said simply. His seductively probing stare made her pulse beat faster. She forced herself to look away, noting that a belly-dancer in full—or lack of full—costume, was entering their section of the restaurant.

Bret followed Charly's gaze, gave the exotic, dark-haired woman a summary glance, and turned back to Charly. "Now, *that's* boring," he told her, as the music swelled behind him. "Ancient stomach exercises in endless rotation." He shook his head.

"I don't know," Charly said, unable to tear her eyes from the sensual woman's impressive, and artfully obscene, gyrations. "She's doing some pretty amazing things."

Bret turned briefly again, gave the dancer another cursory once-over, then returned his attention to Charly. "She's talented," he allowed. "So, where were we?"

Charly smiled, noting that the widened eyes of every other man in the room—as well as the narrowed ones of their female companions—were fixed on the very rotating belly Bret had scorned. But he was apparently more interested in Charly. It gave her a shivery, pampered feeling to once more meet his softly appreciative gaze. Was the wine going to her head? She was starting to enjoy Bret's company much more than she'd thought possible.

The music decreased in volume as the dancer moved across the room. "You were telling me," Bret continued quietly, "about life on the farm. Now, when did you graduate from ponytails, and how have you managed to stay single? You *are* single, aren't you?"

Charly looked at him warily, feeling the beginnings of unease she always felt when she had to think about her marriage—and its end. "I didn't manage," she told him, trying to preserve a light and casual tone. "I got married when I was in college. Now, however—"

Bret nodded, his eyes holding hers. "And now?"

"And now I'm single," she said and looked away. She didn't want to go into the more intimate details. Bret waited, as she'd done earlier when he spoke of his father, to see if she would continue.

The waiter's arrival was a welcome distraction. This man, who delighted in pouring tea from a golden pot held nearly over his head, made a game of creating the longest possible stream from teapot to glass without spilling a drop. They both applauded his performance, and the laughter they shared effectively swept away any more serious conversation.

"How's the ankle?" he asked after they'd sipped the tea, hot, sweet, and delicious.

"Oh, it feels fine now," she said. "Only if I— Hey!"

But he was already lifting her foot beneath the table, propping it up on his thigh. "Does this hurt?" he asked innocently.

All protests died on her tongue, as his strong fingers gently pressed the bare flesh of her ankle, homing right in on a soreness there and softly kneading it. "Umph," was the only syllable she could manage. Thank goodness the tabletop obscured his ministrations from the other diners' view.

"I see," he said, his eyes holding hers. Those lean, muscular hands continued their provocatively lazy caress, sending a warm tendril of arousal seeping from ankle, to knee...

"I wish you'd..." she began, but her tongue had turned to taffy. His hands were gliding higher, molding the soft skin of her calf, thumbs brushing the underside of her knee. *I wish you'd stop,* she finished the sentence in her mind. It seemed an easy enough thing to say. So why couldn't she form those few little words? Because she was thinking, really, *I wish you'd...kiss me?*

Was she losing her mind?

"Very tense muscles you've got here, lady," Bret murmured. If he didn't let go of her leg immediately, she was going to melt.

"It's from chasing chimpanzees," she said with an attempt at breeziness. "Thanks, that's quite enough."

But her leg was still prisoner. His hands paused, lingering at her knee. "Are you sure?" he asked, his voice softly teasing. She wondered if he could feel her skin pulsing to vibrant life beneath his hands, if he could read the whirling, ambivalent thoughts behind her riveted eyes.

Yes ... no ... yes?

Don't let him—let him ...

The dreamlike setting wasn't helping at all. While tambourines jangled and the strange sound of mandolins twanged in the distance, the colors of the smoky room seemed to swirl before her eyes. If he didn't stop looking at her like that, touching her like that, she would let herself lean forward, as he was leaning. She would trace the curve of his sensual lips with her finger—or she would close her lips over the tanned dimple on his jutting chin ...

Mesmerized by his glimmering gaze, she watched his lips part as if in slow motion, only inches from hers now, as his hand rested on her knee, her baggy pants bunched up about his wrist. When had she last let a man seduce her in a restaurant? When had a man last made her feel so breathlessly aroused? When—

"Hey, chief!"

The unfamiliar squeaky voice jolted Charly out of her trance. Sitting back abruptly, she pulled her leg from Bret's grasp.

"Hey, chief! You're running late!"

Turning, Charly found herself staring into a pair of inquisitive brown eyes that peered out from under a baseball cap's visor and a disheveled mass of bangs. The eyes blinked, looked from her to Bret and then back again.

"All right, Smith," Bret grumbled. "Say, how'd you get in here?"

A pair of scrawny shoulders shrugged, and a dirt-smudged thumb jerked in Charly's direction. "You said to come get you. Who's she?"

"Smith," Bret said, sighing. "Mind your manners, not that you've ever had any. The lady's name is Charly. Charly, meet Smith."

The boy, who didn't look a day over ten years old, was dressed in a faded denim shirt, grass-stained jeans, and sneakers. He gave her a wary look and shoved his hands into his pockets. "Hi," he mumbled.

"Hello," Charly said, smiling at the boy's awkward attempt at macho nonchalance.

"You better get back up there," Smith told Bret, pointedly ignoring Charly. "Casey's gonna blow his stack."

"He likes to," Bret replied calmly. "All editors do. Okay, Smith, want to make yourself useful? Find our waiter and have him send the check over."

"Gotcha, chief," Smith said, turned abruptly, and whizzed down the aisle.

Bret chuckled ruefully, a fatherly fondness in his eyes as he watched the boy run off. Charly saw that look and felt a sharp pang inside her. "Who is he?" she asked.

"Smith is sort of the *S.F.* mascot," Bret explained. "His dad was our chief proofreader when the magazine first began, and he died a few years ago. Smith was always hanging around the office, even back then—he was only six or seven. Anyway, we kind of adopted him—or he adopted us." Bret chuckled. "He runs errands for the staffers."

Charly nodded, looking over her shoulder to the far end of the room, where Smith was tugging at a waiter's sleeve. Her heart gave a little squeeze at the earnest, officious expression on the young boy's face as he directed the waiter to their table. "You don't mean legally adopted?" she asked, turning back to face Bret again.

"No, he lives with his mother," he told her. "But after

school he comes straight to the office, and we let him have the run of the place. He helps with the xeroxing, and sometimes one of us will take him out for dinner. But don't worry—he makes minimum wage." Bret smiled as their waiter approached, check in hand, Smith marching behind him like an officer minding a captive prisoner.

"Tell Casey I'm on my way up, short guy," Bret said, giving Smith's baseball cap an affectionate tug. "Go on, scoot."

Smith straightened his cap with a look of great annoyance, nodded at Bret, and gave Charly one more curious glance before shuffling off. Charly watched him leave, trying to relax the ball of tension swelling up inside her. She still couldn't get used to it—that strange void in her life . . .

"I'm glad you got to meet Smith," Bret was saying. "He's pretty special to us. He's at the age where he's not so crazy about the opposite sex, but he'd like you—I'm sure."

Charly forced a smile. "Doesn't he have a first name?"

"Sure, it's Thomas," he told her, taking out his credit card. "But at the magazine we all call each other by last names. He insists we do the same with him."

He bent over the bill, chuckling, and Charly watched him, unable to keep herself from thinking what a fine father Bret Roberts would make. She stifled a sigh and tried to think of other things, but all that came to mind was her doctor's appointment the following afternoon. Involuntarily, she crossed her fingers under the table. That appointment symbolized some new hopes for her. Maybe things could still change . . .

"We're all set," Bret said, breaking into Charly's reverie. "I'm sorry to leave so quickly," he said, rising from the table as she did.

"That's all right," she assured him as they began walking down the aisle. She forced a laugh. "I was only staying for a snack anyway, remember?"

"I'm glad you stayed longer," he said, ushering her
through the arched doorway. Quite suddenly, it seemed,
they were out on O'Farrell, in the cool night air. Charly
pulled her sweater closed, shivering involuntarily as the
wind rose.

"Maybe you need this," Bret said wryly, holding up
his leather jacket.

Charly smiled, shaking her head. "No, I'm fine," she
said. "And that was only good for one round."

"One round wasn't enough," Bret protested quietly,
his eyes holding hers, gleaming with unabashed desire
in the soft light of the street lamp.

Charly swallowed nervously, taking a step back. Her
throat felt taut, and she stiffened as his hand reached out
for hers. "Thank you for the dinner," she said, trying to
affect a casual air. Her heart was beginning to race again.

"You're very, very welcome," he said softly, gently
but firmly pulling her toward him. "You know, if I didn't
have to run off, I'd take you home."

"No, you wouldn't," she said, her voice husky. "Bret,
don't . . ."

But as she pulled back, looking up to meet the bright
blue flames that danced in his eyes, she knew it was too
late. Any protest she might have summoned up was
smothered as his mouth covered hers.

His lips plundered the tender fullness of her own, and
a sense of delicious warmth overcame her as she fitted
her body instinctively to his. Her eyelids fluttered shut.
She leaned into the kiss, delighting in the silky, moist
feel of his tongue gliding over hers.

Some inner, subconscious voice was registering each
intimate detail with unabashed delight. Perfect lips, it
murmured. Soft, fine hair, ideal for running fingers
through. Fantastic skin. Fine, huggable torso . . .

And then even that voice was quieted. She was awash in a liquid pool of voluptuous sensation as two tongues circled, teasing and then thrusting to meet with even more fervent force. She was swaying under the hypnotic massage of his powerful hands as they molded and explored her every curve beneath the flimsy fabric of her shirt.

A tiny groan of passion came from deep inside Bret's throat. Someone—it had to be her—answered with an equally ardent moan. He began tracing the V neckline of her shirt with the tip of one finger, then more forcibly pulling the material downward. A stubborn button gave way, then another, and his hand dipped to gently, tantalizingly cup one lace-covered breast.

She could feel his male strength against her thighs, feel her own center giving way, moist heat unfurling within her as the kiss deepened. And she could feel her heart beating beneath his softly caressing palm. Little shooting stars that weren't in the sky fired off in the velvet darkness. Her eyes were shut tightly, and only when she heard him say her name in a ragged, husky whisper, did she open them again.

"Charly," he repeated softly. "This isn't so bad, now ... is it?"

She gazed up at him dumbly. Bad? It was wonderful. She hadn't felt such an aching, hot desire, such a sweetly savage pleasure, since ... ever. But that was terrible. This wasn't at all what she had wanted to happen.

A distinctive, urgent whistle suddenly sounded from down the street. Bret's eyes flicked from hers to briefly scan the sidewalk. "To be continued," he declared, frowning. "Another kiss like that and I'll lose my job."

His lips brushed her forehead, and then suddenly she was released. She stood there, blood pounding, body weak, and watched Bret Roberts sprint away into the darkness.

Another kiss like that and she'd lose her...everything, Charly thought hazily, trembling in the rising wind. Another few hours with a man like that around, and God knows *what* would happen!

Chapter

4

"THERE YOU ARE!" Trudy peered anxiously over the counter as Charly hurried into The Sanctuary. "I was starting to wonder."

"Sorry, Trudy," Charly said, dropping her bag by the register. "I had a doctor's appointment after lunch that took a bit longer than I expected."

"Are you all right, dear?"

"Oh, I'm fine." Charly gave her a bright smile. "Just a routine checkup." She moved past Trudy to the coatrack, not really wanting to discuss her visit to the clinic.

Making the appointment was something she'd forced herself to do, after reading about the clinic in Mr. Heart's column. Apparently San Francisco was at the forefront of research in the area that concerned . . . her condition, as she termed it. And this new medical center was administering tests that hadn't been available before. Since the move, with her determination to make a fresh start on every level, Charly had decided to give herself—and her body—the benefit of the doubt. The two doctors that had treated her back home had come to contradictory conclusions. Now she wanted to know, for sure, if there was any hope . . .

"You're just in time to give Robbie a hand," Trudy broke into her thoughts. "He's about to tackle Harold's first bath."

"Rob's never done a bath," Charly reminded her, glad to ease back into the distractions of life at The Sanctuary. She wouldn't be getting the results from the lab for nearly a week, so she might as well put the whole issue out of her mind for a while.

"That's right," said Trudy. "So would you show him what's what? I'll take care of the phone and counter."

"Any calls while I was out?"

"No *important* calls," Trudy said with a meaningful look.

Charly rolled her eyes and headed for the little office in the back where she could change into a smock. She knew Trudy was concerned—as was Charly, though she pretended otherwise—that Bret Roberts hadn't called or come by since their date.

For a fleeting moment, as she slipped out of her dress, Charly allowed herself to dwell once again on those smoldering smoky-blue eyes. Thoughts about Bret had been hovering about her all morning, though she tried to brush them aside. She was better off not seeing him, she told herself. The man was trouble, and she should be relieved that he'd abruptly abandoned his flirtatious pursuit.

After buttoning the white smock over her bra and panties, she faced the mirror and took out her lipstick. Forget about it, she instructed herself, then paused, the gilt tube at her lower lip.

Could kisses leave invisible imprints? That lasted forty-eight hours? Why, as she traced the outline of her lips, did she have to relive the gentle velvet brushing of his lips over hers, a quiver rippling from mouth to knees at the vivid memory?

Frowning, she ran a brush through her hair, then exited, determined to end these schoolgirl daydreams by engaging in some practical work. When she pushed open the back door to the patio, Robbie was standing by the portable tub, trying to ignore Harold's hands waving in his face as he bent over the hose. The little backyard was serenely quiet, except for the soft chirping of unexotic birds in the trees.

Harold sneezed.

"Bless you," she muttered, motioning for Robbie to keep a firmer grip on the chimp's arm.

"I'm not sure he likes it here," Rob muttered. "He's been awfully lethargic since that guy left. Kinda depressed, I'd say."

Charly nodded. She hated to admit it, but she could almost say the same thing for herself. "Well, let's see how he likes some fun in the tub." Robbie stepped back as she examined the little unit, quickly and efficiently checking the spray attachment.

"I think I've got everything," Rob said, indicating an array of shampoos and medical soaps in a tray on the cart.

"You do," Charly said, straightening up. "Okay, you just keep holding him in place there. Watch me." She turned the spigot and ran a little stream of water over the back of her hand, adjusting the temperature until is was just right. "Warm but not hot," she told Robbie. "Make sure you test the water like this first. Cold water can get your eyes scratched out if you're bathing a cat; and water that's too hot is just as bad."

She nodded as Robbie put his hand out, feeling the water temperature. Harold was watching everything with great curiosity, not struggling in Robbie's hold. He pursed his fat lips, a sagely patient expression on his hairy countenance.

"How's it going?" Trudy leaned out the back doorway.

"So far so good," Charly said.

"I take it you haven't read Mr. Heart today," Trudy said.

"No. Why don't you go get it? You can read it to me while we do this."

Trudy gave her a peculiarly apprehensive look, then nodded slowly before disappearing into the store again.

"I think it's right," Robbie said after fiddling with the spigot awhile. "Now what?"

"You give the animal a preliminary wetting down before you put the shampoo on," Charly instructed, and she cautiously lifted the nozzle, spraying Harold's feet lightly. The chimp hooted, executing a little two-step, but as he got used to the feel of the warm water he quieted again, and Charly was able to wet him without any problem.

"He likes it," Robbie noted.

"Most do," Charly said, smiling as Harold unceremoniously sat down in the small tub, arms crossed behind his head. "Here, I'll hold him while you give it a try."

She passed the nozzle and hose to Robbie, keeping one hand on the chimp's shoulder. As she watched the young man gingerly spray Harold's back, Charly again found her mind wandering, out of the yard, over the shop, across the street: she was sitting on a tree stump in a small clearing next to a devastatingly handsome man whose eyes shone with sunlight as his face bent to hers...

"Here we are," Trudy announced, coming through the back door again, newspaper in hand.

"Go ahead," Charly said, keeping a watchful eye on Robbie as she held Harold in place.

Trudy wet her lips, held the paper up, then lowered it, looking at Charly over the top of her bifocals. "Maybe *you* should read it," she said in an oddly meek tone.

"Hands full," Charly said. "You go on. I'm all ears."

Trudy cleared her throat, paused, and then began to read. "'Dear Mr. Heart: A friend of mine met a handsome man today who's obviously wild about her. She is a beautiful divorcée who insists she isn't interested in men at all. But when he made a pass, within minutes of their meeting, she certainly seemed to respond. I know my friend has a fear of involvement, but don't you think she's wrong to deny her feelings?'"

Charly stared at Trudy in utter dismay. "Go on," she said tersely, her throat suddenly dry.

Trudy swallowed. "The phone's ringing," she noted.

"You're not moving," Charly said warily. "I want to hear the rest of this letter. Robbie, I'll take the hose. You go in."

Robbie shrugged, complied, and sauntered through the door. Trudy came over to the tub, looking terribly uneasy. "Maybe you should read it yourself, dear," she said in a tremulous voice.

Charly grabbed the newspaper, shoving the hose into Trudy's hand as Harold, seemingly content, splashed the water gently around him, looking from one woman to the other.

"'My friend insists it was the fault of the man's monkey. You see, he came to her pet store—'" Charly stopped, her eyes widened in disbelief. "Good Lord!" she exclaimed. "You didn't leave out one juicy detail. 'My friend says she doesn't want to see him again. I think she's making a big mistake. What's your opinion? Yours, Mother Hen'!" Charly dropped the paper. "Mother Hen?" she cried. "I'd say you were a nosy, interfering—!"

"Charlotte!" Trudy exclaimed.

"Did I ask you to do this?" she fumed. "No! And for goodness sake, you might as well have written my name in capital letters."

"Please, Charly, take it easy," Trudy cried, looking

wretchedly guilt-stricken. "Who will ever know besides the two of us? Do you think Bret Roberts is the sort of man who reads advice columns?"

That stopped her momentarily. "Well, I doubt it," she allowed grimly. "But that's not the point. You ought to be ashamed of yourself, going behind my back and—"

"I am ashamed, I am," Trudy said, looking artfully contrite. "But really, dear, there's no harm in it. Don't you want to read what Mr. Heart has to say?"

Charly stared at her. "Well, of course I do," she grudgingly admitted.

Trudy chuckled. "Of course you do," she echoed.

"I still think you're—" Charly began, but less vehemently.

"Take a look, dear," Trudy prompted, a satisfied look on her face. Charly sighed and picked up the paper.

Dear Mother Hen:

It sounds as if your suspicions are well founded. The heart has its own logic, and I'd say your friend isn't listening to hers. If she felt nothing for this man, why didn't she get rid of him immediately?

I think she needs to examine her romantic reluctance. Painful divorces can lead to more painful solitude. It's time for her to test the waters. Why not give the guy the benefit of the doubt and go out with him again? Then, if she decides she really doesn't like him, she'll at least have expressed her feelings before overruling them.

Yours,
Mr. Heart

Charly noticed the column's logo, a black and white silhouette of a man's profile encased in a heart. She looked up to see Trudy's eyes fixed expectantly on hers.

"I still say you're a busybody," Charly muttered, but

her tone had softened. She knew, despite her embarrassment at this public disclosure, that Trudy had only been trying to help. "You wrote this that very night, didn't you?"

Trudy nodded. "Of course I didn't realize you were going to have dinner with him," she said apologetically. "I thought you meant it when you said you weren't interested in him, period."

"I thought I meant it, too," Charly admitted ruefully. "But my feelings are still there, and apparently begging for expression."

As was Harold, she noticed, tightening her hold on the chimp's arm. He was obviously beginning to feel left out of things. Charly motioned for Trudy to move the hose over, as she checked the water's temperature.

"Trudy, there's a delivery guy on the phone who needs to ask you about bird feed," Robbie said, leaning out the back door.

"All right, dear," Trudy said absently. "Here, you take this." She handed the hose to Robbie, wiping her hands on the towel hanging from the side of the cart. "So, then you agree with us?" she asked Charly, pausing at the door.

"With who?"

"Mr. Heart and me," Trudy said. "You would go out with him again, wouldn't you?"

Charly frowned. "If he asked me, I'd consider it," she said wryly. "The jury's still out. But from the looks of things, he's already forgotten about me."

"Impossible," Trudy said. "He'll call."

Charly shrugged. As the door slammed behind Trudy, she looked back to see Harold bending over the side of the tub. Robbie was squeezing shampoo out while he held the nozzle still aimed at the chimp's feet. "Careful," she cautioned her assistant. "Don't let the spray—"

It was then that disaster struck. Robbie, eyes on the

gob of shampoo in one hand, inadvertantly squirted the curious Harold in the face. The chimp howled, and even as Charly made a grab for him, he kicked at her and lurched away.

Robbie cried out, uselessly, his slippery, shampoo-filled hand no deterrent to the wily chimp's escape. Charly lunged for Harold as the tub tipped over. But Harold, emitting a high-pitched giggle of excitement, jumped onto the cart. And as Robbie tried to grab hold of the chimp's flailing arms, the mischievous monkey responded by squirting a shampoo dispenser at the hapless assistant's face.

Robbie clapped a hand to his eyes, forgetting he was already holding a handful of shampoo. As he yelped in pain, losing his balance, Harold sprinted from the cart to the tabletop again. Charly nearly got a grip on one hairy leg. But Robbie, half-blind and wholly disoriented, got his foot entangled in the rubber hose and brought the entire cart crashing down in front of her. With a shriek, he landed on his rear in a hail of shampoo bottles as Charly stumbled back—and Harold sprinted blithely from table to nearby tree branch.

Hooting delightedly, the chimp clambered along the branch, once more eluding Charly as she strained and stretched on her tiptoes below him. "Harold!" she called plaintively, but the chimp paid her no heed. He was already swinging his way to another branch, headed out of their little backyard area and over the fence to the adjoining courtyard.

"I'll go," she called to Robbie, who was flat on his back at the moment anyway. There was a gate in the fence, fortunately unlocked, and Charly hurried through it to the block-long courtyard that lay beyond the shop's back patio.

Charly shivered in the thin, white smock she'd thrown on over her underwear. She'd planned to be outside for

just a few short minutes, and the smock was only to
protect her from the suds—not the brisk autumn breeze.
At least the sun was shining, cutting through the chill.
And if she could catch Harold before he got through the
courtyard—

No such luck. The wily chimp was way ahead of her.
Even as Charly rushed forward, Harold dashed across
the yard, and around the side of the house at the end of
the block.

When Charly reached the sidewalk, heart pounding
and mouth dry, there was no sign of the chimp. Anxiously
she scanned the street. There, at the top of the hill, a
little hairy figure was speeding around the corner. Charly
took off in hot pursuit.

The rapidity of Harold's escape and the unswerving
direction his flight was taking, made Charly wonder if
he actually knew where he was going. Was that possible?
Harold wasn't pausing at corners or zigzagging back. He
seemed determined to reach some particular destination.

Ignoring the curious looks of passers-by and the cold
air cutting right through her flimsy smock, Charly ran
onward, trying to keep the chimp in sight. Now he was
loping quickly past rows of gaily painted Victorian houses
and rounding another corner as the street sloped more
steeply. Though Charly was getting used to the hills of
San Francisco, she wasn't used to running up them at
such a fast clip. Winded, she slowed as she reached the
top, calling out Harold's name.

The chimp ignored her, advancing steadily up a side
street where the incline was even steeper. Sighing, Charly
followed, hugging herself against the rising wind. Now
Harold was nearly at the top of this hill, where the earth
appeared to end, opening on a bright blue void. The cars
on either side of her were parked at angles that seemed
to defy gravity.

Harold paused at the top, silhouetted against the empty

sky. Then he turned abruptly and scampered up the steps of the multi-gabled Victorian to his left. As Charly watched in dismay, he disappeared around the side of the porch. Legs beginning to ache, she employed her last spurt of speed, and was rewarded with the shocking sight of Harold climbing through an open window.

Charly dashed up the steps and hurried, panting, down the long verandah. She peered into the dark window, and there was Harold, dimly visible just below her. She reached out, hissing his name—and was suddenly blinded by flourescent light.

Four men were seated around a little conference table a few yards away. Their heads swiveled to stare at her as a fifth man, hand still hovering by a light switch on the opposite wall, chuckled softly, his eyes twinkling.

"Welcome, mystery guests," Bret Roberts said expansively.

"Roberts, are these friends of yours?" The man at the head of the table was eyeing Charly, who had one knee up on the windowsill, and Harold, who was scampering over to Bret, hooting happily.

"Hey, fella," Bret said, ruffling the chimp's hair. "Too impatient to use the front door, eh?"

"Are you coming in or out?" Another man at the table rose politely as Charly hovered uncertainly on the windowsill.

"I'm . . . I . . ." Charly paused helplessly, staring at Bret, who was striding across the room, Harold in tow.

"It's providence," he crowed, extending his hand. "I was just thinking about you and here you are. Come on, Charly, you might as well climb in."

The other men were rising from the table, stretching, one shutting off a slide projector and another lighting up a cigarette. Charly glanced around the room, taking in the screen set up before her, the cups of coffee, the table strewn with papers and folders.

"I've interrupted you," she apologized, feeling her cheeks burn as he helped her over the sill. "I had no idea—"

"We were ready for a break," Bret said, his strong arms lifting her onto her feet inside the room. Harold was clapping his hands over his head, drawing chuckles from the men as they headed for the door, talking amongst themselves.

Charly smoothed her smock over her thighs, feeling her skin tingle from his efficient and intimate grasp. Bret's colleagues seemed surprisingly unfazed by the sudden appearance of woman and monkey into their midst. The door swung shut behind the last of them, and then she was alone with Harold and Bret.

Gazing up in some befuddlement at Bret's bronzed and faintly smiling face, she asked, "Where am I?"

"*Omnibus,* West Coast office," he said. "Coffee?"

"No, thanks. I . . . didn't come here to socialize."

"I can see that," he murmured, his smile deepening. His eyes swept her figure in the partially translucent smock with an appreciative gleam in their azure depths. "You look a little like a nurse in an adult movie."

Charly cleared her throat. "I was giving Harold a bath," she explained, crossing her arms in front of her. "He ran away. Apparently he remembered how to get back here."

Bret nodded. "Your phone's unlisted," he said abruptly. "Why?"

"What?" She looked at him. "Oh . . . I just . . . decided not to list it when I moved into my new place." Bret was frowning, as if she'd deliberately been hiding from him.

"I called you at the store, too, the few times I was able," he went on. "But I managed to get busy signals on each try. I've been in San Diego."

"Oh," she said, realizing as she stared at him that he was sporting a few days' growth of beard. He looked tired and haggard. "Are you working on a story?"

Bret nodded. "Fending off a lawsuit," he said ruefully. "We were about to publish an article on an environmental agency that was using protected land for government tests—but the government got testy with us. I've been sitting in small rooms talking to unfriendly people practically since I saw you last. It's good to see you again," he said quietly, giving her a tender look. "I've been seeing you in my mind's eye for days now, but it's nothing like the real thing."

Charly didn't reply. She didn't know what to say. She only knew that she was feeling abnormally lightheaded, relieved, almost giddy with sudden well-being. He hadn't forgotten her. He'd missed her. And she'd been missing him, she realized, strange as that might seem. After all, she barely knew the man.

"You were next on my agenda," Bret said. "Right after this slide show. But now you're here." He chuckled, shaking his head. "Harold's good for something after all."

The chimp was investigating the slide projector, hunkered down on the tabletop behind them. Bret left Charly's side briefly to shoo him off, then turned back to face her. "What are you doing between nine and ten tonight?"

"I'm—nothing," she said, the words spilling out before she had time to think. "But—"

"We could meet for coffee," he interrupted. "Where would you like to go?"

Charly stared at him. She was about to decline the abrupt invitation with some lame excuse, but Mr. Heart's words suddenly came back to her. Why not test the waters? he'd said. She was supposed to listen to her heart, wasn't she? And she couldn't deny that even now, as Bret stared at her with an expectant look on his handsome face, she could feel her body vibrating subtly like a struck tuning fork. There was a special spark between them, she could feel it. Instead of running scared, why not . . . ?

Test? The word acquired new resonance as she considered it. So, he wanted to get to know her—Well, she'd give him that chance. It should be interesting to see how a man like Bret Roberts reacts to two cats, a dog, various birds, and other animals for company, a devilishly perverse imp was whispering in her inner ear.

"Maybe you'd like to have some home-brewed coffee," Charly said slowly.

Bret's eyes lit up. "Fantastic idea," he said. "Am I dreaming, or are you actually inviting me over to your place?"

Charly gave him a wry smile. "Well, I'm assuming that if you have to leave at ten, I'll be relatively safe."

"Relatively," Bret drawled. "You're making me a very happy man."

Well, she mused silently, as he got out a pen to take down her address, let's see how long you stay happy.

The doorbell chimed at five after nine, and the musical cacophony of Charly's home menagerie responded in full voice. Smiling, she pressed the front door's buzzer, and listened for Bret's footfalls on the stairs.

The teakettle was simmering, the coffee beans ground. She wore a simple, flower-patterned shift that was comfortable, attractive, but not figure-hugging. The place was neat, but not *too* neat—she wanted Bret Roberts to experience Charly Lynn at home, uncosmeticized. If he was really seriously interested in her, then he wouldn't be fazed by the clutter of bric-a-brac she'd already collected in her short stay.

If the man couldn't accept a woman who was a certified pack rat, that was just too bad. Roy had always nagged her to throw out her things—the magazines, flyers, posters, antique knickknacks and toys she routinely accrued. Now she was enjoying the luxury of filling up her own little home with as much "junk"—his term—as she liked. San Francisco was a great town for memorabilia collectors.

A chorus of howls and meows greeted the knock on her apartment door. Charly unlocked the door, shooing the curious cats away with her foot, and opened it.

"Delivery," said a bouquet of white roses.

Charly let out an involuntary gasp at the sight of the beautiful flowers. "Oh, Bret, you didn't have to—"

"Didn't have to be so old-fashioned?" he said, peeking around the side of the bouquet. "I couldn't help myself. Well, are you letting us in? I'm as thirsty as these roses."

"Oh, of course," she murmured, ushering him inside. The cats scattered as she closed the door behind him, though Godfrey, her baleful-looking cocker spaniel, sniffed at Bret's pants leg with friendly interest. Charly took the flowers and hurried into the kitchen. "Make yourself at home," she called over her shoulder.

A sneeze was Bret's only answer. Charly glanced back at him as she got a vase down from a shelf above the stove. He was standing in the living room, surveying it with a slightly quizzical air. He'd shaved, she noticed, and though he still looked tired, his trousers were pressed and clean shirt unrumpled. He looked . . . good, she mused, heart thumping.

"You're a Coca-Cola tray fanatic," he observed, examining a pile of the antique trays on the table near the kitchen door.

"You bet," she said, pouring water in the vase.

"I've picked up a few of these at the Sausalito flea market. Ever been there?"

"No," she admitted. The roses really were breathtaking. Charly set them carefully down in the center of her kitchen table.

"You'll love it," Bret said, then sneezed once more, loudly, despite his best efforts to control the twitching of his reddened nose.

"Is it the cats?"

"I'm afraid so," he admitted, looking around him warily.

"Maybe this isn't the best place to have coffee, then," she said, pausing in the act of pouring the boiled water over the grounds.

"I'm sure I can handle it," he said, screwing up his face in a comic attempt to ward off another impending sneeze.

"Just open a window. That one'll help," she added. "Ricky and Lucy don't sleep in here, so it's the room most free of cat hairs."

Bret opened the window and hovered close by it, stoically insisting he'd be fine. Charly returned to the stove and prepared their coffee.

"You don't look entirely moved in." He was peering through the bedroom door.

"It's true," she said. "There are still big boxes of stuff I haven't even touched."

"You didn't move the fish from back East, did you?"

"No." She laughed. "New acquisitions. And the dog as well."

Bret sneezed again. "Charly?"

"Bless you. What?"

"Am I hallucinating or is there a rabbit under your bed?"

"His name is Dennis," she informed him, coming over to the doorway. Bret looked up at her from his perch by the window.

"What else?" he asked wryly. "Should I be on the lookout for a stray boa constrictor?"

"No," she said. "You've met the whole family."

A sing-song tweeting from the hall—Scarlett, the parakeet—contradicted her. "Well, give or take a few," she added.

Bret shook his head, then leaned over to take a deep breath of the cool night air. At last he rose and approached the table. "Coffee smells great," he said.

"Have a seat," she offered as she brought over two mugs. Coffee poured, she sat down opposite him, feeling somewhat nervous in the silence. Bret pulled a candleholder toward him on the tabletop.

"Are these for show or can we use them?" he inquired.

"Well, if you'd like . . ."

Bret nodded, pulling a lighter from his pocket. He lit both of the long white candles that Charly had been saving for some unspecified festive occasion, got up briefly to douse the kitchen light, then sat down again. The white roses glowed in the soft candlelight. She realized that his impromptu setting of the scene had imbued her little kitchen with an alluringly intimate atmosphere.

"Cheers," he murmured, raising his coffee mug. Charly smiled, then sipped her coffee as he sipped his. "Good," he pronounced, leaning back in his chair. "It suits you," he mused, appraising her across the table. "Candlelight and roses." His eyes held hers, the flickering candle reflected in their soft blue depths. "Of course, wine would be more appropriate, but I'm still a working man."

"You're going back to work at ten?"

"Around then," he said.

Charly shook her head. "Which job is it tonight?"

"The newspaper," he said, dismissing it with a blithe wave of his hand. "But I'm on a break now, Charly." He leaned forward. "Let's hear about you. What have you been up to these last few days? I want to know everything."

Charly laughed self-consciously. "You'd fall asleep," she joked.

Bret shrugged. "All right, then tell me about the past few years."

Charly looked at him warily. "Is there something more specific you're interested in?" She glanced at the kitchen clock. "You've got about forty minutes."

Bret smiled. "I'd like to hear more about why you left Massachusetts," he said quietly. "And your marriage."

Charly met his eyes, then looked away. "Well," she said, "I'll give you the outlines. I met Roy Mifflin when I was in college. I was a junior, and he was a senior with a promising career in computers ahead of him." She paused.

Bret was still watching her, patient and expectant. Charly sipped her coffee, stalling. This wasn't at all the way the evening was supposed to be proceeding. Bret was supposed to have balked about the animals, winced at the apartment, and exhibited some defective character trait that she could pounce on as an excuse to end their relationship before it began. So far, no luck.

"We never really wanted the same things," she said, wrapping up four years in one simplistic phrase. "I guess I'd rather not go into the whole mess," she added apologetically. "If it's okay with you." What she'd left out already could fill a book: how she'd wanted a family, how he wasn't ready, and how her need for children had come between them, and then . . .

Bret nodded. "All right," he said simply. "But just out of curiosity, what was it you wanted?"

Charly looked down at the table. "Oh, you know," she said with a little sigh. "Old-fashioned stuff: a family, a home, security." She looked up at Bret again. Now here was a man, she reflected, whose footloose and fancy-free lifestyle outstripped Roy's by miles. He couldn't even settle down and work in one place! She was willing to bet anything that the items she'd just listed were at the bottom of Bret Roberts's list of priorities. "Of course, you Californians are a lot more progressive," she joked. "I can't see you being tied down by such . . . commitments."

Bret leaned back in his chair, casually kicking off his

loafers with an ease that she found simultaneously unsettling and oddly arousing. "Actually, Charly," he said
slowly, "you've just named the very things I care about
most."

Charly stared at him, startled, and he held her look.
There was no doubting the sincerity in his eyes. She
cleared her throat as another negative expectation evap-
orated beneath his steady gaze. "You can't mean that,"
she said lightly. "You're always on the run."

"And tired of it," he said quietly. "I'm just about ready
to make a serious commitment, if you want to know the
truth. I'd love to be able to work in one place, live in
one place, settle down with the one woman who means
the world to me and raise a family."

Charly gulped down the knot in her throat and took
another sip of coffee. This was not what he was supposed
to be saying. None of the other men she'd dated in this
town would admit to such goals. Maybe Bret really was
different. It was an unsettling thought. "Well," she said,
"that's . . . interesting. More coffee?"

Bret chuckled softly. "Charly, I have a feeling you'd
prefer to keep the conversation light. Am I correct?"

"Maybe so," Charly said, avoiding his penetrating
gaze as she rose to refill their coffee cups.

"All right, then," he said amiably. "Seen any good
movies lately?"

Charly shook her head, smiling. Bret certainly was
disarming. By the time they'd finished a second cup of
coffee, he had coaxed her into a spirited discussion of
their mutual likes and dislikes in music, books, and films.
Their conversation was punctuated by an occasional sneeze
and some sudden silences when they merely looked at
each other in the candlelight. Charly could feel the elec-
trical attraction between them with palpable force.

When Bret looked at his watch with a sudden exclamation, she was caught completely off guard, having

been lulled into a surprising state of well-being. Never having dreamed she could enjoy his company this much, she was dismayed to discover that she didn't really want him to leave.

"Say, Charly"—Bret was looking under the kitchen table with a perplexed expression.—"any idea where my left shoe might be?"

"Oh!" She looked at him, chagrined. "Godfrey. He likes to hide shoes. It's probably in the bedroom."

She walked quickly through the doorway and snapped on the light, letting out a startled cry as the bulb blew out with a flash.

"Wait a second," Bret said, taking a candle from the table and following her into the room with it. "Here you go."

Charly bent down to peer under the bed. "He usually hides them here," she said. Bret sat down on the end of the bed, resting the candle on the mattress beside him. Charly found one shoe by feeling around, and then the other. Bret sneezed. "Bless you," she said, presenting the shoes. But Bret didn't put them on.

"Charly . . ." His voice trailed off as he gazed at her. "Come here," he said softly.

She went to him, drawn by the husky promise in his voice and the inviting look in his eye. Bret took hold of her hand and lightly kissed the center of its palm, causing a little shock to run through her from head to toe. "Yes?" she said in as casual a voice as she could manage.

"Charly, I have a feeling you remembered about my allergy to cats." He was still holding her hand as he looked at her. "I even have a crazy feeling you only invited me here because you thought I wouldn't want to stay."

Charly swallowed nervously. "But that's ridiculous," she said. "Why would I want to deprive you of a cup of coffee?"

"Because you know damn well I didn't come here just for coffee," he said firmly.

"I do?" She knew she must seem quite transparent.

"If you are trying to get rid of me, it's not working," he said. "We've got too much to talk about, you and I, and too much to share."

Still holding her hand, he rose from the bed, face clenched to stifle another sneeze. Charly could feel both a tug of sympathy for his condition and an uncontrollable urge to laugh. "Are you okay?"

"I will be," he said grimly. "Because I'm not leaving just yet. I'm not going to let you sabotage this night." His eyes smoldered with undisguised desire. "For us, it's only beginning."

And then, before she could pull away, he drew her into his embrace. His soft, supple mouth touched hers with feather lightness, and then he began to nibble erotically at her lip. As she felt his fingers moving through her hair, it was she who increased the urgency of their kiss.

A hot flush of excitement surged through Charly, filling her with fiery desire. She didn't think to question it. His mouth drank in the sweetness of her parted lips, his tongue teased hers, and she sank into the heady arousal of billowing passion. She could feel her breasts straining against his chest, his hands slipping possessively down her back to pull her even closer to him.

Her arms locked around his neck, and her mouth hungrily claimed his. The rough heat of his demanding tongue inflamed her all the more. She moaned as he molded her pliant body to his, his hands smoothing the curve of her hips and buttocks. She felt a sudden release of the tension that had been building up in her all night. Red-hot sparks seemed to dance over her skin at his urgent touch, and firelight danced behind her tightly shut eyes.

The warmth of spiraling desire rose from deep within

her as she felt the evidence of his arousal against her thighs. Her heart was pounding at a dizzying rate as his searing hot lips softly covered hers. She felt herself melting in langorous surrender...

...and realized, dimly, even as she felt Bret suddenly stiffen, that the firelight dancing behind her eyes was no mere illusion. The air was filled with an acrid odor, and a fire was truly burning—on the sheets of her bed!

She staggered back as Bret dashed forward. She saw him silhouetted against the flames, beating a pillow against the bed. In a matter of moments the room was plunged into darkness again. As she hovered close by, Charly could hear Bret's continued efforts to beat out the smoldering sheets, accompanied by his rhythmic whispered curses.

"I've heard of things getting hot and heavy, but this is ridiculous," he said as she began to giggle helplessly.

"That was exciting." Her giggle turned to a cough. Godfrey started barking.

"God, I'm sorry, Charly," he said. "I never should have let that candle sit there unattended." He coughed, sneezed, and then sighed.

"Bless you," she said, the smoke stinging at her eyes.

"I'm going to have to wet down your mattress," Bret muttered. "In fact," he announced. "I'm going to have to get you a new one."

Chapter

5

"THIS ISN'T NECESSARY, you know," Charly protested.

"It's the least I can do," said Bret. "Try that one."

Charly glanced surreptitiously around the vast mattress display. There weren't many other customers in Magnin's bedding department during this particular hour, but she still felt supremely self-conscious. She reached out a tentative hand to test the firmness of the mattress beside her, then sat down on it.

"What do you think?"

Charly shrugged. "It's too hard."

"You like them softer?" Bret asked. "Me, too." Eyes twinkling, he sat down on the mattress.

Charly promptly got up. "Besides, it's too expensive," she told him.

"Don't worry about it," Bret said, also rising. "How about that one over there?"

Charly cast a wary eye at the queen-sized bed he was indicating, then felt her stomach sink. A smiling salesman was on his way over, evidently eager to help his only customers.

"It's a supra-firm beauty-rester," the man announced, heading her off en route to the bed. "On sale." He was a naturally beaming, fatherly type, and he was looking from Charly to Bret with a knowing air, as if they were all sharing some delightful secret. "Go ahead, young lady," he boomed. "Give it a bounce."

Charly, lips tight, sat tentatively on the edge of the mattress. This one was indeed softer, but at the moment she felt too embarrassed to ponder its fine points. The salesman was standing by Bret, arms folded, and both men were looking at her expectantly. Bret's faint smile betrayed some perverse enjoyment at her discomfort.

"Don't be shy," the salesman urged. "Lie back. You want to be sure about an investment like this one."

Charly put her hands down on either side, testing the bed's springiness, wishing she'd never agreed to this little field-trip. But Bret, confronting the hole he'd burnt in her mattress, had refused to take no for an answer. He'd insisted she meet him at the department store the following day. The mattress would be his treat.

She got up, glad to see that the two men were now involved in a discussion of firm versus soft, and the care of one's back. She moved on to another row. Away from Bret's watchful and amused eyes, she felt free to try out the next mattress more enthusiastically. This one gave beneath her weight but felt firm enough. She stretched her legs out and dug her elbows in. Not bad.

"That looks comfy." The men were back. Charly straightened up. "And you, sir?" the salesman asked Bret, as Charly rose from the bed.

"That's okay," Bret told him, his eyes holding Charly's. "Whatever the lady wants."

The salesman smiled in evident approval of this gentlemanly attitude. Charly wondered if it would be possible to sink through this particular floor and materialize elsewhere.

"I'll take this one," she mumbled to Bret.

"You're sure?" His eyes had a mischievous glint. "There are quite a few you haven't tried."

"It's fine," she said. "I'm not sure about the size, though."

"Oh, we have this in a number of sizes," the salesman interjected. "Full, twin, queen, and king."

"Full is fine," Charly said.

The salesman looked startled. "You don't want the queen?" Again he glanced at Bret.

"Don't worry about cost," Bret repeated earnestly. "Comfort is what counts."

"The king is on sale," the salesman said helpfully.

"What am I going to do with a king-sized bed?" Charly said, exasperated. Then she wished she hadn't. Both men regarded her for a long moment.

"The queen isn't too big for your room," Bret said at length, as the salesman stepped back in a rare show of discretion.

"I suppose," Charly said with a sigh, and glanced at her watch. "Let's just get this over with. I've only got a few more minutes." She was due back at the clinic for the preliminary results of her tests. The prospect was making her unusually tense.

"Okay," Bret said. "If you're sure you like that particular mattress. You'll be using it for a long time, you know."

"Yes," Charly said dryly. "*I* will. Let's take it."

The salesman guided them to a desk. Bret took a seat, handing over his credit card, and the man started filling out forms. "Delivery address same as the billing?" he asked.

"No," Bret said. "Charly?"

The salesman looked from Bret to Charly again. As Charly began to recite her address, she felt her face reddening. In one short minute, her imagined status in the salesman's eyes had shifted from newlywed to . . . mistress, probably.

As the man started making phone calls, Charly checked her watch again. "I've got to run," she informed Bret. "Thanks. I really do appreciate this."

"I thought I was the one who was always running out," he said. "I was hoping we could have lunch."

Charly shook her head. "No . . . Just have them call me about the delivery date, okay?"

"And when is *our* next date?" he asked, stepping closer.

Charly felt her heart starting to shift into high gear again. Whenever his soft blue eyes caressed hers at close range, she felt the warm tension rise between them and cloud her thinking. "We'll—talk," she said hurriedly, and backed away.

"Soon," Bret murmured. The wistful look of unfulfilled desire she saw in his eyes stayed with her six escalators down.

As soon as she got home from work, Charly raced through the task of feeding her animal family. It had been a busy afternoon in The Sanctuary, and she'd had no time to mull over everything Dr. Halloran had told her, let alone examine the papers the kindly endocrinologist had given her.

Once the kitchen was quiet but for the sound of happy beasts at dinner, she sat down at the table, the brochure and the printout of her medical chart spread out before her. She read the material carefully, examined the chart for the third or fourth time, then sat back, frowning, as she tried to remember the doctor's exact words.

One phrase came back with ringing clarity, and she repeated it, mentally, reveling in the sentence's implicit optimism: In fact, Dr. Halloran had said, 50 percent of infertile women treated *are* able to achieve a pregnancy.

Fifty percent? Even women with histories like hers?

Yes. Even after two miscarriages, there was a chance.

But the doctors back East . . .

Well, those doctors had come to conflicting conclusions, after all. Charly had been wise to investigate further. And if her current . . . partner was willing to come in for testing as well . . .

Charly smiled ruefully, folding up the brochure. "Current partner." That was California for you. And there was the ironic rub. To really continue with her case, the doctor required that she be in the process of . . . well, trying to conceive. And at the moment, of course, Charly wasn't. Far from it.

All in all, the whole experience had been frustratingly inconclusive. For the present, she'd have to be content with the knowledge that her body, which had betrayed her so tragically in the past, still held the potential for motherhood—or so it seemed. Charly sighed, rubbing a hand over her eyes. Had this been pure foolishness, after all? Was she now building up a fragile hope, only to have it destroyed later on?

She closed her eyes, feeling that too-familiar lump swell in her throat. She wouldn't be able to bear another disappointment. The very thought of nurturing those hopes again, of trusting in the unknown, of wanting, so desperately, to fulfill her dream—and then finding out she couldn't . . . The prospect filled her with dread.

And what about the man who might share that dream, as Roy never had? Could she bear *his* disappointment along with her own?

Charly shook her head, pressing her eyes with her palms to stop the tears before they began. No, not today.

She'd had her share of self-pitying moments, and she felt stronger now. It was time to put the whole troubling issue aside. She'd worry about it . . . later.

The doorbell's buzz startled her. Charly got up from the table and pressed the intercom. "Yes?"

"Delivery for Charlotte Lynn."

Shrugging, Charly buzzed the downstairs door open. She wasn't expecting anything. She unlocked the door and peered out at the sound of sneakers squeaking on the stairs.

It was Smith. Dressed again in his dirt-smudged jeans, T-shirt, and ubiquitous baseball cap, he came chugging up the stairs, a brown-papered package under his arm. "Hi," he grunted, as he reached the landing.

"Hello, Smith," Charly said, smiling "What's this?"

"I dunno." He held the oblong package out, avoiding her eyes. "The chief said you needed it." He thrust it into her hands, apparently ready to bolt down the stairs again.

"Hey, Smith," Charly said quickly. "Do you have any interest in some chocolate-chip cookies? With a glass of milk to chase them down?"

His large round eyes met hers for the first time: "Soft or hard?"

Charly smiled. "Soft."

Smith shrugged. "As long as they don't have raisins. I hate raisins."

"Come on." She ushered him into the apartment.

"Wow," he muttered, "what a lot of junk! This is neat!"

Charly left him in the living room, bent over Dennis the rabbit, and poured him a tall glass of milk. When he'd met all of the animals and was happily wolfing down cookies at her kitchen table, Charly unwrapped the package.

The sheets were silvery-white and made of pure satin. She felt a little shiver go down her spine as she ran her fingers over the sinfully luxurious material. "This is too much," she murmured, staring at the matching pillow-cases in her lap.

"Just a bunch of sheets," Smith observed disparagingly. "What's the big deal?"

Charly cleared her throat, gathering up the wrapping paper. "Tell Bret—the chief—that I like his style," she said.

Smith nodded. "The dude's cool," he allowed.

Charly looked over at the boy, supressing the urge to reach out and wipe the little white film of milk from his upper lip. Her heart gave a wrenching tug as she watched him carefully remove an unwanted walnut from the side of another cookie.

"I understand you do some work at the *S.F.* office," she said.

Smith nodded with an air of satisfied importance. "Sure," he said. "I run the Xerox machine. I know how to fill the ink and change the paper and everything. I do it better than Mrs. Waller." He grimaced. "She's the office manager. I could do her whole job better than she does," he said.

"I'll bet you could," Charly said soberly, as Smith's eyes searched her face for any sign of doubt.

"It's a breeze," he said. "When I grow up, I'll be an editor there. Boy, that would be fun—me bein' the one to give the chief a hard time every day!" He flashed her a toothy grin.

Charly smiled, rising to answer the ringing telephone. "There's more milk in the fridge," she told him. "Hello?"

"Charly." Bret's voice caressed her ear. "Did you get your delivery?"

"Yes," she said, turning her back to the boy at the table. "Bret, you really didn't have to..."

"But aren't you glad I did?"

Charly smiled. "I've never slept on satin sheets," she admitted.

"Me neither," he said blithely. "But I thought that

once you'd got the hang of it, I might wheedle an invitation."

"Keep dreaming," she said, but the smile stayed on her face, and she felt a ticklish warmth of arousal billowing inside her as a stream of provocative images came unbidden to her mind.

"Smith come and go? Tracking mud through your immaculate abode?"

"Is that supposed to be a dig?" she joked. "No, he's still here."

"Then he's either eating the entire contents of your refrigerator or torturing your cats," Bret guessed.

"Just milk and cookies," she corrected him.

"How wholesome!" Bret chuckled. "Around *S.F.*, he's always trying to sneak sips of coffee or beer. Charly, you've got the makings of an excellent mom."

The smile faded from Charly's face. She swallowed, glad he couldn't see her expression. "Not necessarily," she disagreed.

"Seriously, hanging around you would be good for that little demon," Bret went on.

Charly forced a little laugh. Of course, he had no way of knowing how his words were affecting her. "I'm just giving him cavities," she said, trying to disguise her discomfort. "Do you want to speak to him?"

"No," Bret said. "I want to see you—as soon as possible."

Charly exhaled deeply. "Oh," she said, stalling. "But we're both so busy—aren't we?"

"I'm never too busy to pursue a certain breathtaking green-eyed beauty of perfect curvature and silken skin—"

"Stop, stop," she said. "Save it for your articles."

"I want you to have dinner with me," he said. "In an animal-free environment. With more than an hour to spend. I was thinking of my place. Or does that prospect frighten you?"

"Only a little," she admitted. "Don't tell me you cook?"

"Decently," he said. "So, what do you say to a home-cooked meal? No strings attached."

Charly paused. "Meaning?"

"Meaning I promise not to force you into any position you're absolutely sure you don't want to be in," he said gently.

Charly bit her lip, the warm feeling blooming inside her like hot air filling a balloon. "I suppose you're an honorable man," she murmured.

"Completely," he said. "How about tomorrow night?"

Charly took a deep breath. "I think this is where I'm supposed to say I'm all booked up, such short notice, et cetera."

"But you won't say that," he assured her, and she could picture the tiny smile lines crinkling at the corners of his bright blue eyes. "You'll ask me how to get to Sausalito."

"Sausalito?"

"Right," he said quickly. "You go down to the Golden Gate Bridge—"

"Wait, whoa." She laughed. "I still haven't said yes."

"Charly," he said in a grave voice. "I'm making tacos. That's California cuisine. It's your duty as a new resident to grab every opportunity to imbibe the native foods—"

"Okay, okay. Let me get a pencil."

His directions would lead her to a dock on the Sausalito bay, because Bret, she learned, actually lived on a houseboat. It was one more detail in the continuing unexpectedness of Bret Roberts, and she dutifully copied down his detailed instructions, then read them back, at his insistence.

When she finally hung up the phone, Charly turned to find Smith eyeing her warily.

"The chief can't cook to save his life," he said. "If you're going out to the boat you'd better eat before you go."

Charly smiled. "You've had dinner there?"

Smith nodded. "Now and then. But we get take-out." He got up from the table, wiping his mouth with the back of his hand. "Thanks for the cookies," he said gruffly, then paused. "Hey, you don't need the rest of them, do you? I mean, there's only a few, and the guys at the office . . ."

"Sure," Charly said, unable to resist giving his baseball cap a little tug. "Take them for the guys at the office."

"I'm sorry we couldn't come up with better weather for you," Charly said, turning on her windshield-wipers as they approached the bridge. Her companion said nothing, but grinned happily, his spirits obviously undampened by the dark, drizzly sky.

Bringing Harold to Sausalito had been Trudy's idea. She'd noted that the chimp had been severely depressed, cooped up in his cage, and hadn't been eating. Charly, happy to have a chaperone of sorts, and an excuse to return to San Francisco before very late—she had The Sanctuary keys, and would bring him back on her way home—agreed that some fresh air and a visit with Bret would do Harold good.

He already looked perkier, seat-belted into the VW beside her. Charly was the one whose spirits were in danger of deflating as she drove onto the bridge. She was having second, third, even fourth thoughts. Bad weather. Bad night for tacos. A myriad of absurd reasons to turn back flashed through her mind as the drizzle turned to a stronger rain.

The one that lurked behind all the others was the worst, though, because it was real. She didn't need a Mr. Heart to tell her why she was so afraid of getting involved with Bret Roberts. Because what if it did turn into something serious? What then? What would happen when he found out she couldn't have children? Why should she get involved with any man . . . under the circumstances? Wasn't that just asking for trouble?

For Bret Roberts wasn't like Roy Mifflin in one important aspect: Bret wanted children.

Sighing, Charly turned on the radio. Harold hooted happily at the strains of country-western music and Charly smiled, unable to dwell on maudlin thoughts with a monkey beating mock-time on the dashboard at her side. She began to hum along, glancing at the directions she'd taped to the dashboard. She was now in Marin County. The docks should be coming up on the right soon.

There they were. The rain was temporarily abating, and she could see the line of yachts and sporting boats, their silver masts piercing the cloud-heavy sky. The bay was full of them, though none were at sail. She drove slowly, parallel to the dock as Bret had instructed. His boat was apparently moored down at the farthest end.

The rain began again just as she caught sight of the boat he'd described. It was long, battleship gray, and bargelike. A jeep was parked just across the dock from it. Did Bret drive a jeep? Its plain, masculine lines matched his no-nonsense personality, she decided. Charly pulled into the space beside it and turned off her motor, glancing at her watch. She'd allowed too much time for the trip into Marin County and was twenty minutes early, but she doubted Bret would mind. In any case, she wasn't going to sit here with rain drumming on the roof until the stroke of seven-thirty.

Charly got out, pulling her slicker around her, and hurried around to Harold's side. She got him unbelted and hoisted in her arms, shut the door with her foot, and quickly hurried toward the dock. The rain chose that particular moment to come beating down with renewed force.

Harold wriggled excitedly in her arms. As she carefully stepped over the roped mooring and onto the deck

of the boat he bolted from her grip and raced to the doors
that led to an inner cabin. He looked up at her, then beat
on the bottom of one with his fist. She shook her head,
amused by his impatience to be reunited with Bret. When
there was no answer, she knocked herself on the slick
wooden surface.

From outward appearances, the houseboat was un-
distinguished and rather spartan, if large. It reminded her
of the jeep Bret drove. When he didn't answer her knock,
she tried the doorknob, emboldened by the downpour
and Harold's whimpering. The door was open. Relieved,
she slipped inside.

As her eyes adjusted to the soft light, Charly gasped.
Her slicker was dripping onto the edge of a beautiful,
thick, Persian rug, which extended into a long living-
room area anything but spartan in its decor. The walls
were a dark mahogany with gleaming brass fixtures, and
only the room's narrowness suggested she was on the
water and not Nob Hill. A black velveteen couch and an
antique writing desk stood near an old oak file cabinet,
drawers open, beneath a *Casablanca*-style wooden fan,
blades slowly revolving on the low ceiling. The room
was at once entirely masculine and subtly refined.

It also suggested a level of wealth and taste she hadn't
suspected Bret Roberts of possessing. She called his name,
then turned suddenly as Harold went scampering down
the narrow hall ahead. Charly hurried after him into
another room, pausing hesitantly in the doorway. The
small bedroom housed a beautiful brass bed, a night
table, and little else.

Above the steady beat of rain, she heard the sound of
slightly out-of-tune whistling coming from an adjoining
room. Louder running water indicated a shower. No wonder Bret hadn't heard her knock. As noiselessly as she
could manage, Charly crept over to Harold, who was
seated happily on the end of the bed, gnawing at a thumb-
nail.

"Come on, fella," she said. "We'll wait for Bret in the other room."

But Harold shook her hand from his hairy shoulder and ran to the other side of the bed. Charly sighed, and leaned over. He hopped away. Annoyed, she counted three, then lunged for him. Still he eluded her, and Charly found herself lying spread-eagled, facedown, across the bed. And that's when the bathroom door opened behind her, and a whistle stopped in mid-melody. Charly whipped her head around and froze, staring.

Bret Roberts stared back at her, his tousled wet hair gleaming in the bathroom's light. His lips relaxed into a welcoming smile. He was amused, unperturbed—and stark naked.

Chapter
6

CHARLY HAD NEVER experienced an electric shock. But this must certainly be what one felt like, she thought dazedly as her entire body pulsed. Her eyes couldn't help but take in every detail of Bret's masculine form. Rivulets of water traced a gleaming path from his wide shoulders, through the blond-haired thatch on his broad chest that tapered down to a flat, trim belly...

She had forgotten how to breathe. She was too busy registering the intimate details of his well-proportioned body, aware of the response of her own body, a response that overwhelmed her in its raw intensity. As her eyes rose quickly, guiltily to meet his, his smile broadened. His eyes twinkled with a knowing look that indicated he considered her inspection only natural.

"Good evening," he said. "You're early—but I'm glad you've made yourself at home."

Charly opened her mouth, but her dry tongue and tightened throat failed her as he made no attempt to cover himself. At last her voice came out in a hoarse whisper. "Do you mind . . . ?"

"Not at all," he said expansively. "Hey, my bed is your bed."

"I mean"—she cleared her throat—"don't you believe in towels?"

"Towels." He snapped his fingers. "Oh, sure. Excuse me." He turned, offering her a clear view of his firm buttocks and muscular back. Charly tore her eyes away and sat up abruptly, feeling that she must be glowing bright red all over. Where was Harold?

"I like your outfit," Bret was saying pleasantly, indicating her raincoat. He leaned against the doorway, a towel now rakishly slung around his waist. "But you are staying awhile, aren't you?"

Charly swung her legs over the side of the bed. "I didn't mean to barge in here like this," she said quickly. "I came to get Harold." She leaned over, peering beneath the bed. Predictably, the chimp was crouched below, hands covering his head, ostrich-style.

Bret shook his head. "Charly, *you* have Harold now. Remember?"

"Come here," she commanded the chimp in hiding.

Harold rolled over, peeking at her through splayed fingers. But it wasn't until the mattress squeaked and she felt Bret sit down beside her that Charly realized she'd been misinterpreted. "Not you," she said sharply, standing up. Her arm tingled where his bare skin had brushed hers.

Bret looked at her, perplexed. "Who else?"

"Harold!" Charly exclaimed, exasperated. "You're practically sitting on him." Bret raised a dubious eyebrow, then bent over. Why, for goodness sake, couldn't she stop looking at the supple musculature rippling under his tanned skin? She was all-too-conscious of the freshly showered, musky male scent of him.

"Harold, old chum, old buddy," Bret was saying, surprise apparent in his tone. By the sudden commotion from beneath the bed, Charly could tell that Harold recognized his master's voice. A moment later the chimp was climbing into Bret's lap, nearly knocking him back on the bed in his enthusiasm.

"Well, this is a heartwarming scene," Charly said. "But I think I'll get out of this wet stuff—in the living room, if it's all right with you."

"Sure," Bret said, his voice muffled as Harold attempted to smother him in an embrace. "I'll be out in a minute."

Charly breathed a shaky sigh as she escaped the confinement of Bret's bedroom. By the time he appeared in the living room, hand in hand with Harold, she was seated demurely on the couch, affecting great interest in a copy of *Omnibus* she'd taken from a pile by the desk.

"Well, this was a fine idea," Bret said, indicating Harold. "It's good for him to get out and exercise, is that it?"

"That's part of it," Charly agreed. "But it's also because he's been absolutely pining for you," she told him. "Lovesick. Trudy says he's on a hunger strike." She laughed at Bret's comic look of incredulity. "She also thought he'd make a good chaperone," she added.

"I see," Bret murmured. He gazed at Charly a moment, long enough for her to appreciate that he looked as sexy in corduroy pants and an ivory alpaca sweater over a button-down shirt, as he did in . . . less.

"Oh, he won't be a bother," she said, breaking the silence. "You don't happen to have any bananas on board, do you?"

Bret smiled. "I'll take a look. I should be in the kitchen, anyway." He walked down a few steps into a small galley fully equipped with stove, sink, counter, and portable oven, all compacted into a cupboard-lined enclosure.

As Charly ambled over for a better look, Bret straightened up from his half-sized refrigerator, Harold peering in at his side. "Why don't you do the honors with this, while I hunt up some monkey food?"

She took the bottle of white wine and the corkscrew, and sat on a stool near the steps. "You seem to have everything you need here," she said.

Bret closed the refrigerator. "Nearly everything," he said slowly, his eyes meeting hers again, glimmering with that faintly mischievous look she'd come to know and even enjoy.

"All the comforts of home, I mean," she said playfully, and pulled the cork free. "I bet you've even got two glasses."

"Absolutely." He turned to the cupboards. "Do you think Harold would be satisfied with apple sauce and a couple of nectarines?"

"That'll do," she assured him. "And what do *I* get?"

"Something more substantial," he said, smiling, and took the bottle. He poured the wine into two glasses, and handed her one. "Veal."

"I'm impressed." Maybe Smith had exaggerated Bret's culinary ineptitude.

Bret chuckled, slapping some butter into a large pan on the stove. "Don't be. It's one of the simplest recipes I know. And I only know two."

"Two?" She smiled. "Burgers?"

"Pancakes." He took a sharp knife to a garlic clove, chopping with a careful thoroughness she found oddly endearing. Harold sat contentedly at Bret's feet, plopping nectarine slices into his mouth with great gusto.

"This is even more impressive, though," she mused, looking around at the lavish furnishings as she took her seat on the stool. "Is it all yours?"

"Afraid so," he said, adding garlic to the sizzling hot butter. "My one indulgence."

"It's wonderful," she said, then paused uncertainly. "But maybe you could explain something to me. Why does a man who rides around in an old jeep, who wears faded jeans and corduroys, who works at something like half a dozen different jobs . . . why does someone like that live in luxurious digs like these? I was expecting something more like a bunk bed and a hot plate."

Bret looked at her in silence a moment, apparently in the midst of making some mental decision. "My family's wealthy," he finally said. "I've struck out on my own, but there are still some things . . ." He frowned. "This boat was a gift from my father, many years ago." He pounded the veal with what looked to her like unnecessary vehemence as he continued: "It was really intended as a bribe, to be absolutely truthful. But I welshed on my end of the deal."

"Which was?" she asked.

"To stop all this writing and running around and join the family firm. Follow in my grandfather's footsteps.

"What's the firm?"

Bret chuckled ruefully. "Well, that's the irony of it. My father's a newspaperman—on the management side, of course. *His* father owns them, lots of them. It's a regular empire." He looked at her over his shoulder. "Hubert Foster Roberts. You know the name?"

"That Roberts?" She stared at him. Of course! she knew the name of that legendary tycoon. The idea that Bret came from such a wealthy background sent a little shock wave through her. Bret was watching her carefully. Charly did her best to mask the fact that she was momentarily overwhelmed. She intuited that he disliked being perceived as a scion of the idle rich.

"Yes, that Roberts," he said with a faintly rueful smile. "And my father takes after Granddad, in a serious way.

To him, writers are a lower form of life. He sees papers and magazines as commodities, period; never mind whatever nonsense gets printed in them—as long as the stocks go up." He shook his head, turning back to the sizzling pan. "He's never been good at understanding people," he mused. "Only products."

Charly sipped her wine thoughtfully, seeing Bret in a new light. It couldn't have been easy for him to go against the family grain. A lesser man might have reaped the rewards of a trust fund—surely he had one, then?—and never worked at all. But apparently Bret had made a clean break, entering wholeheartedly into the workaday world. She felt a twinge of admiration for the unpretentious man bent over the pan in front of her. And sympathy . . .

"Do you speak to your father?" she asked quietly. "Does he know what you're doing?"

"I suppose he keeps tabs on me through the grapevine," Bret said. "And I guess I'm always trying to send messages to him, indirectly. A lot of Grandfather's papers—the ones Dad manages—print trash; so I try to do quality. Some of his magazines pay high prices for the lowest kind of gossip-mongering; so I work for the ones who pay worse for better journalism. And I've been able to support myself doing it, which is a thorn in the old man's side."

"Is that why you free-lance for so many publications?"

Bret nodded. "And I've been learning the business from the other side, too. In fact, I'm just about ready . . ." He paused, then shook his head. "Never mind. Do you like broccoli?"

Charly nodded absently. "You're ready for what? To . . . "? Bret's eyes met hers. "To start your own paper?" she guessed.

Bret held her gaze a beat longer, then shrugged. "It's something I've thought about for years," he admitted.

"A publication with good articles about real issues." He stopped suddenly. "Now, don't get me started," he cautioned. "I'll talk your ears off and the veal will burn. More wine?"

"Thanks." She extended her glass, her mind still somewhat dazed with these new perceptions. So this chimp-chasing man in jeans was . . . rich? Or rather, abstractly rich . . . an heir? Good Lord, what would someone like Trudy say if she knew Charly had been fending off a man like—

Like what? Charly frowned slightly, sipping her wine. Her image of Bret was changing again. It deepened every time she saw him. And the better she knew him, the better she liked him. He was a regular guy, tycoon-grandfather notwithstanding, and he lived a life that was his own—unique. And though the idea of dating a man who came from money had its superficial attraction, she knew there was more to Bret than that. But why was she even thinking this way? What difference did it really make? It wasn't as if things were serious between them, she reminded herself.

As he finished cooking the meal, Bret coaxed Charly into talking more about her own work and told her a bit about his. By the time they were seated, it felt perfectly natural to laugh with him and tease him about his cooking, which was actually quite good. She put all thoughts about his past—and their future—behind her, and concentrated on the food.

"The pine nuts are a nice touch," she told him, savoring a forkful of the broccoli and wild rice dish he'd concocted. "Your own invention?"

Bret nodded. "That laugh of yours is wonderfully musical. Trained?"

Charly smiled, shaking her head. "I couldn't hold a tune in a sieve. But then, neither can you."

Bret opened his mouth to protest, then stopped. His

memory of how she'd come by that information registered in his glimmering blue eyes just as she remembered,
herself. The vivid image of his towelless appearance in
mid-whistle only an hour before brought a flush to her
cheeks. She looked to the porthole, bringing her napkin
to her lips and avoiding his amused gaze.

"It's cats and dogs out there," she commented, to
break the awkward silence. It did seem as if the rain was
more forceful than ever.

Bret nodded, then glanced over the table toward the
kitchen. "Speaking of which, where'd Harold disappear
to?"

"I didn't notice," she said, putting her napkin down
and starting to rise. Bret waved at her to stay put. "My
gourmet meal will get cold," he said. "He can't have
gotten into too much trouble, wherever he is."

Charly shrugged. "I'm happy to keep eating," she told
him. "But I don't know if I should keep drinking," she
admonished him, as he prepared to pour her a glass from
a newly uncorked second bottle.

"Why not?" He paused, bottle hovering. "You seem
perfectly sober to me." He smiled as she raised her eyebrows. "Or rather, you seem perfect to me, and close to
sober."

Charly shook her head. "I don't think so." She reached
for her glass, but in attempting to pull it back, succeeded
only in knocking the lip of the bottle. Some wine splashed
into her glass.

Bret chuckled. "Changed your mind?"

"No, I'm just clumsy," she said. "But another drop is
okay, I guess."

"Your subconscious changed it for you," he asserted,
refilling his own glass. Charly stared at him, his words
reminding her of Trudy's letter to Mr. Heart. Her pulse
rose a notch as a second wave of pure paranoia swept
over her. He couldn't possibly have . . . But then, he *was*
a newspaperman.

"So, what do you think of the San Francisco press?" she asked, in what she hoped was a casual tone.

"Not much," he said. "In my opinion, the North Beach *Voice* is the only one worth reading, and that's a weekly."

"But you said you wrote for some of the local papers," she prodded.

Bret sipped his wine, swallowed, then said: "Oh, yeah, now and then. But the *Tribune* has the edge, I'd say. Better sports section."

"Oh," Charly said, then took the plunge. "I read the columns in the *Sun* sometimes, just for fun." She watched him carefully for a reaction, but his face remained impassive.

"To tell the truth, Charly," he said at length, "I'm usually too busy writing to read any more than the headline stories and the sports."

Charly breathed an inward sigh of relief. Of course, it was an absurd idea, anyway, that Bret Roberts would read an advice column like Mr. Heart's. Her secret was safe. She took another sip of wine, the tension ebbing from her tightened muscles.

Then, peculiarly, as she put her glass down, the table moved. Or was it the floor? Bret met her startled gaze with one of his own. "That's weird," he muttered, rising abruptly from his seat and hurrying past her.

Charly followed him, thoroughly alarmed. Was she about to experience her first San Francisco earthquake? Bret pushed the door open. She hung back in the doorway, stepping to one side as a spray of rain blew into her face.

"Dammit!" Bret cursed loudly in the uproar of the torrential storm. Charly peered through the mist, but couldn't see anything in the gray darkness around them.

"Why, you little . . ." She heard Bret's sharp intake of breath. She could only dimly make him out, bent over the side of the deck. She heard a whimper and howl, unmistakably Harold's, and then the rain-drenched chimp was running toward her, hands clapped over his ears. She tried to grab him, but he brushed past her, running inside for cover. Charly stepped out onto the deck, too curious to worry about the downpour.

Bret was crouched by the back of the boat, a coil of rope in his hand and a scowl on his face. He looked up at her, shaking his head. "Our little friend found some trouble to get into, all right." He spoke loudly over the continuous clatter of rain on the deck. "He's unmoored us."

"Unmoored? You mean—"

"We're adrift," Bret said, sounding more annoyed than worried.

"What'll we do?" Charly cried. "Don't you have engines on this thing?"

Bret shook his head ruefully. "They're down—out of service. We're not prepared for sea-going."

"Sea-going?" Charly gasped. She had a sudden horrific vision of them floating out into the Pacific.

But Bret was smiling, "Don't worry," he called, motioning for her to follow him back inside. "Come on, you're getting soaked."

Heedless of the rain, she grabbed at his sleeve, panicked, as he rose to go in. "Wait! What do we do? Are we in danger?"

"No," he soothed, taking her arm. "We're on the inmost inlet of the bay here. I've still got one anchor down, and the worst that can happen is we drift into another boat."

"But that's terrible!"

"Charly," he said reassuringly, "the wind's going to blow us right back against the dock if it gets any stronger. We'll probably just float around in a wide circle with the anchor for ballast. There won't be any fast-moving boats out in this weather anyway. Come on!"

Charly let Bret pull her back into the main cabin. Only

when he'd shut the doors firmly behind them did she begin to shiver. The light gray cotton shift she'd worn was now a dripping black, and she was soaked to the bone.

"Towels," Bret muttered, hurrying past her toward the bedroom. She stood where she was, gazing at her reflection in the mirror: streaked makeup; wet, moplike hair—she looked like a water rat. Great. Fantastic. And she was stuck on this boat with Bret Roberts, for . . . how long?

Then he was back, one towel draped around his shoulders and another thrown over her head before she could protest. Strong hands tousled her wet hair as she flailed for control of the whizzing yellow cloth.

"Hold still!" he commanded, and she gave in with a sigh. His hands were efficient, warm, and firm as he toweled her head and neck. Then the yellow cloth zipped past her eyes and she was staring, a little dizzy, into his.

"I'm not going to be responsible for you catching pneumonia," he said. "So you'll have to get out of those clothes."

Charly stared at him, a knot forming in her stomach. "But—"

"I've got a robe you can put on," he said with a wry smile. "So don't give me that look. We have an agreement, remember? You're in the hands of a gentleman."

Instinctively, she glanced at his hands, still lightly grasping her trembling shoulders. Bret dutifully removed them. "This way, madame," he instructed. He was as soaked as she was, she noted, following him back to the bedroom.

Once inside, he opened a cedar chest and motioned her to go ahead into the bathroom. "I'll dig something up for you," he said. "Get out of those things and dry off."

Charly shut the door firmly behind her. With a sigh

of resignation, she unzipped her shift and stepped out of the dripping garment. At Bret's knock, she grabbed the nearest towel, holding it up like a shield as she stood there in her wet underwear.

"Here we go," he said, the door opening a crack. A hand appeared, offering a black terrycloth robe.

"Thanks," Charly said, taking it. The door shut. After a moment's deliberation, she chose comfort over modesty and removed her underwear as well. She slipped quickly into the warm, thick robe, which was way too big for her, belting it tightly. Then she took a few futile stabs at her hair, gathered up her wet things and tentatively opened the door.

Bret was nowhere in sight. She was about to go look for him, when a rustling noise beneath the bed stopped her in her tracks. Charly knelt down and found Harold crouched below as he'd been before. The little chimp was curled up in a ball, apparently in the belief that as long as he couldn't see her, she couldn't see him. Charly smiled and left him there to be contrite.

She hadn't noticed the old-fashioned Franklin stove in the far corner of the living area when she'd first arrived. But Bret was standing in front of it now, having lit a fire in the stove's belly.

"It gets cold in the winter, even in Sausalito," he explained. "I'll just hang these—"

"I'll do it," she said. She draped the shift over a wooden stool, which Bret placed on the other side of the stove. He was wearing a man's Japanese-style kimono, in a blue and white print that served to make his lustrously tanned skin glow darker in the fire's light. "Now what do we do?" she asked, gazing into the flames.

"We eat dessert," Bret suggested. "And we drink coffee, or tea, if you'd like. And we continue our talk, which I was thoroughly enjoying before we got so rudely interrupted."

Charly smiled. "I was enjoying it, too," she admitted.

"But then what, I mean; how do I get back to shore?"

"You don't," he said simply. "Not in the dark, in a storm like this. No, we have a little pajama party, that's all." His eyes lingered appreciatively over the robe. "I've got pajamas, if you want 'em."

Charly's throat was suddenly dry. "But . . . I can't," she protested.

Bret shrugged. "I think it's out of our hands," he said quietly.

His gaze held hers, the reflection of the flames flickering in his soft blue eyes.

"I suppose it is," she murmured. And then with a sudden recklessness, she said, "And I guess that's not the worst thing in the world."

Bret's eyebrow lifted in pleased surprise, the line of his mouth relaxing into a smile. "No," he agreed, "that's not the worst thing."

For a moment they merely looked at each other, a little current of arousal shimmering in the air between them, a silent acknowledgment of it passing from his eyes to hers. A piece of wood snapped suddenly in the fire, and she dropped her gaze, stepping back.

"I'll put on the coffee," Bret said. "Unless you'd like—"

"Coffee's fine," she assured him. Suddenly feeling acutely awkward, she drew the robe tighter around her and turned to watch the fire. So she was spending the night, then. The thought sent a delicious tremor rippling down her spine.

Charly walked slowly back to the table, where the remains of their dinner lay, and picked up her wineglass. She downed the rest of it in a single gulp.

"So, tell me about your paper," she said when he'd joined her by the table, sipping the rest of his wine. "The one you said you'd been thinking about starting. Are you really ready to do it?"

Bret stroked his cheek thoughtfully. "I'm working on

the financing," he said. "It's a little early to go into details."

"What sort of a paper would it be, though?" she persisted, curious.

"You really want to know?" She nodded. "Well, it would be similar to what the *Voice* was, years ago: rebellious, full of vitality, open to all opinions, no matter how crackpot they sounded . . ." Bret smiled. "No articles on what the movie stars eat for breakfast, no gruesome black-and-white photos of crime and punishment . . ."

As he served them coffee, and a plate of sinfully rich cookies baked by a local Sausalito bakery, Bret talked and Charly listened—more to the fervor in his voice that revealed his love for the city and its history, than to the specifics he unraveled. She watched the sparkle in his eyes shine even brighter, and realized that his own excitement was buoying hers. The more he talked, the more she wanted to hear him. And during it all, his eyes held hers, seeking her reactions, savoring her opinions and taking them seriously.

When the coffee was over, Charly insisted on doing the dishes. He walked with her to the sink, hovering close by as she washed, talking, smiling, making her smile.

The rain beat down and the fire blazed. It seemed to her there wasn't any world outside, only the two of them adrift in the velvet darkness she glimpsed through the portholes. And even standing there in his oversized robe, with her hair still a mess and her hands full of soap and dishwater, she felt . . . pretty. And Bret's admiring glances told her she was. The sensation was both unusual and oddly natural, as if she was re-learning something she'd already known a long, long time ago.

When Bret's hand grazed hers, his eyes sweeping briefly across the bare nape of her neck as he reached for a brandy glass in the cabinet beside her, she knew suddenly what it was he was making her remember. It was the experience of being womanly, feeling admired and sexy, not as an object or plaything but as herself. He was admiring the inside Charly, the one she'd been so shy of showing for so long.

Brandy glass in hand, she followed Bret over to the little stove. They sipped quietly, watching the flames, listening to the howling of the wind and the steady beating of the rain above them. When she looked up at him, realizing they'd been silent for some time, there was an invitation in the smoky depths of his eyes that was unmistakable. For once, she didn't force herself to turn away.

Their gazes locked. Another log popped, and only as a spark shot from the stove to her robe's hem did he look down, his hand brushing the material just below her knee. She shivered slightly at the casual contact, and Bret straightened up slowly, staring into her eyes again.

His hand reached out to gently stroke her cheek, fingers tenderly playing with a wisp of hair around her ear. Again Charly felt the simmering desire that had been building up inside her all evening, as Bret's eyes silently posed an unspoken question.

Instinctively she wet her lips with her tongue, the warmth from his finger's touch fanning the flame that seemed to burn within her as brightly as the fire before them. The feeling swelling up in her was impossible to ignore any longer. He watched her, waiting. How could she deny wanting him?.

The incandescent glow of his eyes held her still, even as she thought to move away. Her hand stole out to arrest his, as the delicate touch of his fingertips on the soft skin of her neck provoked another shiver. But instead of pushing his hand away, she found herself, mesmerized, slowly pulling the palm downward, so that his fingers traced the line of her neck and paused finally at the pulse near its base.

His eyes still held the question as he faced her expectantly in the firelight. Her eyes must have given him the answer, or maybe it was her pulse beating so strongly beneath his warm fingertips, because without another word his lips dipped down to meet hers.

Chapter

7

INSTINCTIVELY CHARLY PARTED her lips to taste the sweetness of his mouth, a warm, shivery current of arousal coursing through her from Bret's tender touch.

His mouth left hers, hovering inches away, and without thinking she moved forward, lips still parted, breathless. She saw a smile lift the corners of his sensuous lips, and suddenly embarrassed by her own naked desire, she looked down shyly.

"Bret," she murmured, "I'm not..."

He bent his face to hers, lips brushing each eyelid, kissing the lashes with a tenderness that made her tremble. His hand lightly traced the line of her neck. "You're not...what, sweet Charlotte?" he whispered.

Charly swallowed, the pounding of her blood making it difficult to speak. She wanted to tell him how long it had been since she'd felt this way. But then, she'd never felt this way, quite. Not with Roy, not with any man; never so vulnerable, so openly aching with love and need.

"It's been so . . ." Her halting voice faltered. Bret lifted her chin with his thumb and forefinger, his eyes gazing into hers.

"You don't have to say a word," he murmured. "You've said all you need to say, darling." His lips brushed hers in a feather-light kiss. "Knowing that you want me the way I've been wanting you since the moment I saw you— that's all that matters." His voice was a husky whisper. "We'll go slow. Gently." He kissed her chin.

The erotic promise of those words, the exquisitely light touch of his skin against hers made Charly's blood whirl in heated excitement. Her mouth moved eagerly to his, her hands sliding past his neck to grasp the curls of his fine, soft hair.

As she pressed herself closer to meet him with an uninhibited urgency of her own, Bret's mouth commanded hers with a tantalizingly slow exploration. Now that he had promised to be gentle, to be patient, she felt her own tension release, her own desire mount in an uncontrollable surge.

His body moved sensuously against hers, and a moan started and caught, deep in her throat. Charly slid her hands slowly from his neck to feel the warm hardness of his chest. Their kiss lengthened, and her hunger increased. She reveled in the feel of the curly chest hair beneath her fingertips, playing at the collar of his robe.

She could feel his strong hands gathering her against him, and she shivered as his fingers traced the line of ner spine, then restlessly gathered the folds of terrycloth. She was aware more than ever that they both stood naked beneath these robes. In a single savage moment they could be skin to skin before the crackling flames.

But Bret's fingers dropped the gathered cloth. His hands rose slowly along the curves of her body, and his lips broke from hers. "I love the way you feel in my arms," he groaned.

She smiled, her hands still holding the collar of his kimono while her hips grazed his, and his hands rested lightly at her sides, fingers brushing the swell of her breasts beneath the terrycloth. "I thought you said I needed padding," she joked softly, delighting in his prolonging of this moment, when passion and anticipation made the air electric.

"I can't wait to see," he whispered, his eyes slowly moving from her face to the neckline of her robe, "just how wrong I was."

Now he bent his lips to her throat, planting a hot, moist trail of kisses from her chin to her collarbone. She arched her back, barely able to stand the delicious ache of pleasure she was feeling, and her hips moved instinctively against his.

Bret's hands stole up to part the neck of her robe with painstaking slowness. He kissed each inch of newly revealed skin, bringing it to tingling, vibrant life beneath his soft, wet lips. Tingle by tingle, he kissed a path to the hollow of her breasts, which were partly hidden by the still belted robe.

Charly's mouth half-opened in protest when his mouth left her skin at last. The swollen tips of her breasts were rubbing against the taut cloth, and she was aching for his mouth to claim those aching peaks. But again his lips found hers.

Now, more than ever, though she gloried in the slow, tantalizing build-up of their passion, she wanted to feel all of him against her, unrestricted by clothing.

Then his lips left hers, and his arms gently released her. And as their eyes locked in a wordless communication, his hand crept out to untie her robe's belt at last.

"Mind reader," she whispered.

He smiled. She felt the robe fall open, heard his slow

intake of breath as she reached to undo his sash. Then his hands came up to softly push the shoulders of her robe away. She let her arms fall at her sides, and the soft material slid from her, swishing into a little pile around her feet.

For a long moment he gazed upon her, his eyes drinking in her nudity in the firelight. "Lord," he breathed, his voice ragged. "You're so beautiful, Charly."

Suddenly emboldened, she pulled at the soft material of his robe, her own eyes widening as his body stood revealed before her, silhouetted against the fire.

His gaze lingered on the quivering pulse at the base of her throat, paused to drink in the full roundness of each breast, to savor the line of her taut belly, the roundness of her hips. Then he stepped forward, the tips of his fingers spread to slowly trace each curve, hands moving down from her shoulders. Charly gasped as his hand closed gently over one breast. His palm slowly, lightly circled its swollen tip, sending an exquisite shiver down the length of her body.

She tangled her hands in his soft hair, her back arching. The feelings that surged within her as he kissed and nibbled one breast and then the other, his hand cupping and fondling each in turn, were overpowering. She closed her eyes, her breath coming in ragged gasps. "Too long," she whispered. "It's been too long."

When Bret lifted his mouth from her breast she stiffened, her fingers clutching his hair. She didn't want him to stop. "Much too long," he agreed, in a husky whisper. And then his mouth returned to kiss a fiery, trail down between her breasts, as he bent and lowered himself to a kneeling position before her. His arms slid round her thighs and his hands gently molded the curve of her buttocks as his lips covered the soft skin of her stomach with kisses. His mouth fanned the warm center of her arousal into a white-hot flame.

She shuddered as he tantalized her with playful strokes of lips and tongue. Even when his mouth finally left her trembling skin, her body continued to shake and she clung to him, gathering his warm strength to her with an exultant moan.

They turned, her hands feverishly pulling his body even closer against hers, the slowness of their beginnings abandoned now as passion overtook her. She bent her face to cover his neck and chest with kisses, until it was he who groaned in pleasure. Her hands explored his body, caressing him with tender, teasing touches until he cried out as she had, and thrust her from him.

They faced each other in the dancing firelight, eyes gleaming with unbridled passion. Then, with a deep-throated, wild laugh, he grabbed her, swooping her up into his arms. Aloft again, she laughed, too, her arm around his neck, loving the feel of his nakedness as he swung her gently in his arms.

"You seem to like carrying me," she whispered, smiling.

"It's become a favorite pastime, yes," he said, his eyes alight, grin wide. "But this time I'm only taking you as far as my bed."

"Your bed?" She savored the syllable on her tongue as he carried her across the carpet. "You mean, you're going to tuck me in? Before you . . . retire to the couch?"

"Dream on," he growled, turning in the narrow passageway at the entrance to his bedroom. "I'll tuck you in, all right . . ."

Bret lowered her gently onto the bed, and Charly pulled him down beside her, impatient with desire. When his lips found hers, she returned the kiss with an untamed passion that matched his own. She gloried in the feel of his hard, rugged body, the wonderful roughness of his hairy chest against her breasts.

They rolled together on the big brass bed in a sudden

paroxysm of passion, murmuring wordless sounds of pleasure, as he fitted his body to hers. Only when they sank into a long, deep kiss of breathless urgency did the bed stop swaying and squeaking underneath them—and then a sudden scrambling of feet could be heard.

Charly's eyes flew open, and Bret's head jerked up. Startled, he stared at the bed's edge. A pair of hairy ears emerged, followed by wide eyes even more startled than theirs. As Harold scampered out from under the bed, Charly giggled helplessly, and soon Bret was laughing along with her.

"Our chaperone has flown the coop," Bret announced, his hands sliding restlessly over her skin.

"Not a moment too soon," she murmured. And then his smiling lips swooped to claim hers again.

Their bodies met once more, curve cleaving to curve, skin melding to skin. She'd never known such pleasure was possible; a prolonged, sweetly savage pleasure, it ebbed and flowed, inexorably mounting between them. Time after time, she felt herself being led, panting, to another plateau of arousal, only to hurtle even higher, urged on to still greater heights by his eager lips and hands.

He was tender and demanding; he tortured her with gentleness, soothed her with brutally possessive caresses. She barely knew herself, awed as she was by her own passionate fervor, her own reckless abandon in response to his touch. Had she ever loved before, then, ever given herself over to such feeling? As the teasing, drawing out of each kiss and caress became unbearable, it was she who cried his name, who pulled him to her, arching her body and pressing it more feverishly to his.

"Charly," he breathed. "Do you want me, love?"

"Yes," she told him, with a strangled moan. "I want you . . ."

With an exultant groan he entered her at last. Charly moved sinuously, ecstatically with him, savoring the ex-

quisite feel of his hard strength within her yielding softness. She stroked the powerful width of his back, loving
the feel of his smooth skin. The throb of her pulse min-
gled with his heartbeat.

Together they sought the 'empo, felt out and found
the ultimate beat, their bodies dancing as one atop the
tangled sheets. He teased her still, with knowing gentle
movements, and she answered him in kind, surprising
him and herself with the intimacies they could share.

But soon there could be no prolonging every instant,
every move, no slow drawing from each caress the last
drop of arousal. There was no stopping the gathering
momentum of their mutual desire. She wrapped herself
around him, flying now, climbing, leaving gravity behind. She heard him groan, felt his name being torn from
her lips with each hurtling thrust.

There were words of love in a language she'd never
known as their flight grew more frenzied. Like a fiery
comet, she felt herself hurtle beyond the brink at last,
every fiber of her being stretched taut and singing until
a flaming white spasm sent her heavenward, weightless,
free...

It was the rain she heard first, after the dreamlike
sweetness. Her eyes slowly opened, and she saw Bret's
face before her. She wanted to study every detail of it,
to drink in the loving look in his hooded eyes. Their blue
had turned smoky with a tenderness Charly felt, too. His
taste was still on her parted lips; his body still enveloped
her in sheets slick with sweat. She could have lain there
in his arms forever.

"Hello," he whispered.

She smiled. It was all she could manage. Her body
felt wonderfully exhausted, saturated with satisfaction.
He traced the outline of her half-open lips with the tip
of his thumb.

"I'm memorizing that smile," he said. "With my fingers." Bret closed his eyes briefly, his thumb pausing at the middle of her lower lip, and Charly kissed it.

"Bret," she murmured. He opened his eyes again, fingers gliding softly down her cheek.

"Charly," he said, the smile lines at the sides of his full lips deepening. "Happy to make your acquaintance."

Charly felt a sudden surge of love for this man who'd made her feel so exquisitely a woman. She leaned forward to kiss those little lines at the edges of his mouth, and they nuzzled each other. Like furry jungle animals, she thought to herself, as her tongue flicked out and playfully licked the dimple in his chin.

"I've been wanting to do that for a while," she whispered.

"I've been wanting to do all of this." He sighed happily, kissing her once again. Then slowly, he rolled over beside her, an arm slipping behind her neck. "For eternity, at least . . ." Bret propped his head up, gazing down at her, his eyes shining softly in the darkness. "I knew we'd be good together," he said quietly. "But I never could have imagined *how* good."

She gazed up at him and felt a wonderful warmth spread throughout her body. "How good?" she prompted.

His hand gently cupped her breast, palm lightly pressing the tender ache of its still-taut peak. "Better than I've ever felt in my life," he said simply. "There's only one problem."

"What's that?" She sighed, as the tingling sensations of his deft caress aroused her once again.

"I'm sure that you're addictive," he said gravely. "I'm going to want to feel this way again . . . and again. And I'm pretty sure it'll only get better and better."

"Ummm," she agreed, shivering happily as his finger traced a feathery path from the curve of her breasts to her taut stomach.

"I love the way you feel against me," he said softly.

"I love the way you look when we're together like this. I love"—he planted a warm, moist kiss on the tip of each breast, and then her lips—"you. All of you," he whispered. "Inside and out."

Charly stared at him, hearing the words, savoring them with a distant pleasure. It was as if he were speaking to another woman. She both disbelieved and accepted the phrases at the same time. What did he mean, really? He was probably only being kind, affectionate.

It still gave her a flushed, excited feeling, though, as his caresses grew more tender and he held her gaze, his fingers trailing over the curves and hollows of her body. "You're nice," she whispered.

"Nice?" His eyes narrowed, fingers pausing. She wasn't sure his affronted look was real.

"Well, you're also kind, and warm, and . . . oooh," she breathed, as his hand explored more intimate terrain. "And sexy."

"Glad you added that last one," he muttered. "I thought you were about to say we should just be friends."

Charly sighed, her body beginning to move involuntarily beneath his magical caress. "Too late for that," she whispered.

"I'm having a hard time believing how beautiful you are," he said, as if this was truly troubling him.

Charly laughed. "Keep talking," she said, sweet exhilaration bubbling up inside her.

"You bring out the animal in me," he went on, as his fingers made her writhe in a slow, sinuous motion. "I feel like beating my chest and hollering the call of the wild. But that would require taking my hands off you for a moment, which would be quite impossible."

"Don't," she breathed, her voice a breathless moan.

"Don't what?" he asked, sliding closer, his husky, honey-toned voice tickling at her ear.

"Don't take your . . . don't stop," she moaned.

"Actually," he assured her, "I was just getting started."

It almost seemed that time had stopped altogether. The rain was pattering steadily on the roof above, and darkness still surrounded them. "Are you asleep?" she whispered.

Bret opened his eyes, stretched out beside her in the tangle of sheets. "Can't sleep," he murmured. "I'm too happy."

A stab of longing pierced her core as she drank in his naked masculinity in repose. If time could stop, she'd stop it here. Before she had to think about tomorrow— probably only minutes away—or dwell again upon all her yesterdays . . .

It was the past that seemed unreal now. How had she ever thought she knew what lovemaking was about? But stranger yet, how could she ever have thought all men were like Roy?

Lazily, Bret ran his hand around the swell of her hip, gently pulling her closer to him as he lay behind her. She fit herself into the curve of his body, reveling in the feel of his warmth enveloping her, his arm cradling her breasts.

Roy would never have been this giving, or outspoken. He'd always been so guarded about his feelings. It had taken him months to come right out and admit he loved her. Clearly he felt that real men didn't discuss their emotions. He saw such behavior as a sign of weakness, no doubt.

It was ironic, she mused, snuggling into Bret's embrace, that Roy's unwillingness to reveal his inner feelings had made him seem so romantically mysterious at first. But it was that very quality of his that had helped destroy their marriage. Maybe if he'd been willing to admit what he really wanted, or rather, what he didn't want, things might have been different. Maybe if he'd shared his real feelings with her . . .

But why think about it now? Charly forced herself to stop that train of useless thought. Right now, with Bret's arms around her and that wonderful fulfilled feeling inside her, nothing else mattered.

Closing her eyes, she listened to the rain and felt herself floating in the bay, as if this bed was a raft, afloat on a soft, dreamy sea of contentment...

A sudden jolt awakened her, minutes or hours later. Woozily, Charly sat up, registering the early morning light and Bret's absence from the bed. She smelled fresh coffee, heard a loud banging, felt another minor jolt.

She swung her legs over the bed, suddenly self-conscious as she heard the sound of voices from outside. Her clothes... Frowning, Charly got unsteadily to her feet and retrieved a towel from the bathroom. She went to the bedroom door and cautiously peeked out.

The main cabin was empty, but she could dimly glimpse Bret through the open doors at the far end. He was standing with a coil of rope around his shoulder waving goodbye to someone. Now she heard a motor's engine, felt the houseboat sway slightly. Retrieving the terrycloth robe she'd worn and slipping it on, she hurried over to the stove.

In a moment, Bret reappeared. "Good morning," he called cheerily, reaching her in a few long strides and gathering her to him in a hug.

"What's going on?" she asked.

He kissed her sleepy eyelids and led her over to the table by the window. "Take a look," he said.

She looked. The dock was gleaming in the bright morning sun. "We're safe?" she murmured.

"Peter Kastan helped give me a push and pull with his fishing schooner," Bret said. "We'd only drifted out some forty yards. Coffee?"

Charly nodded, yawned, and Bret stole a kiss as soon as her lips were closed. Blushing, she sat down by the table and watched him move around the little kitchen, remembering how she'd watched him the night before. Now, she reflected, with a warm erotic shiver, she knew about that little mole just above his buttocks, and the way his muscles tensed when he was...

She swallowed, that lightheaded, slightly delirious feeling returning. Bret was coming back to the table with two steaming cups of coffee and a plate of scones.

He ran his hands through her mussed-up hair, then sat opposite her. They regarded each other in silence. She could see the same erotic charge glimmering in his soft blue eyes, could feel the current pass between them. Remarkable. Just sitting mutely at a table with him made her feel as if they were in bed again.

"We don't have to get up, you know," he said, his eyebrows twitching mischievously. "I mean, we could have scones in bed."

"You're telepathic," she said, smiling. "But I'm afraid..."

"... we won't get out of it once we're in?" Bret nodded. "Yes, it's a dangerous proposition."

She couldn't stop looking at him, recognizing her own thoughts mirrored in his eyes. Only Harold distracted her, as the chimp lumbered into the room, a grapefruit in his paw. Bret chuckled as the chimp took a seat on the floor at the foot of the table, noisily slurping his own breakfast.

"It's a little crowded here, though," he said, taking her hand. "Maybe in the back, where there's more privacy."

"Bret..."

"It's Saturday," he reminded her. "And besides, we have important things to discuss."

"We do?" She sipped the coffee, looking up dubiously.

He nodded emphatically and led her out of the main cabin and back to the bedroom, scones in hand. She sat up, tucking the robe demurely about her legs. But he was taking off his clothes.

"Bret..." She shook her head, smiling, then unconsciously ran her tongue along her lips, as he stood revealed before her, then hopped onto the bed.

"This is the life," he cried, stretching out beside her, sipping at the coffee she offered him. "Did you sleep well?"

"I think so," she said smiling. "How long was I asleep? Ten minutes?"

"More like three hours," he said.

"And you?" She couldn't resist running her hand over the soft tangle of hair on his chest.

"Actually, I didn't sleep much at all," he said. "I was thinking." He kissed the soft skin at the crook of her arm. "Thinking lots."

"About what?" She turned to face him on the bed, putting the coffee cup down on the little table. With a growl, he pulled her closer, nuzzling her robe open with his head. She giggled, giving herself over to the warm, moist exploration of his lips, the smile turning to a deep, shuddering sigh as he licked and fondled her breasts.

Abruptly he lifted his head, gazing deeply into her eyes. "About us," he announced. "We have some decisions to make."

She gazed at him, startled. "Such as?"

"It's a gorgeous day," he told her. "We could stay here and laze around, we could go ashore and have a bigger breakfast, we could do both ... or we could start making arrangements."

"Arrangements?"

He nodded emphatically. "For our life together."

Charly stared at him, her heart beginning to hammer with both excitement and apprehension. "But we ... we don't have a life, together ... do we?"

"We do. We will. I'm not letting you get away, Charly." He was speaking in an almost casual tone, but she saw the seriousness in his eyes. "We belong together."

"Belong?" She cleared her throat. "You mean, because of last night..."

"Last night was just a confirmation," he said almost brusquely. Then his voice softened as he added, "No, it was more—much more."

"But, Bret." Her voice had a nervous edge. "We've only known each other a week or so."

"I'm not counting days, Charly, I'm feeling things. And what I feel isn't based on mere time." He cupped her chin, fingers stroking the soft skin of her cheek.

"And what do you feel?" she asked tremulously, almost afraid to hear his answer.

His eyes caressed her face with a smoldering warmth. "I feel it's right," he said quietly. "You and me. I knew when I first saw you that there was something there, and now I know it. I can feel how strongly we...connect."

The intensity of his look was frightening her. She tried to laugh, seeking a way to make light of this. "Connect? Is that a California term?"

He smiled faintly and shook his head. "I'm in love with you, Charly."

This time she knew it was no idle banter. And she knew, as the knot tightened in her stomach, that she was already falling, already in love with him. Somehow the idea was vaguely terrifying. "You don't know me, Bret," she said.

"I know plenty." His fingers traced the outline of her lips. "I've seen you angry and indignant—that was a well-aimed slap, by the way—and I've seen you caring beyond the call of duty." He paused, shaking his head. "Harold doesn't know how lucky he is." He smiled. "I've seen you excited, nostalgic, embarrassed...aroused." His eyes held hers, and a now-familiar tremor started up deep within her. "I know you, Charly," he said softly. "And you're the kind of woman a man would do everything to have, a woman who could be everything to him."

Charly's throat was tight, her mind whirling. The words were all she'd ever dreamed of hearing, but they struck an icy chord within her. She wasn't that woman. She *couldn't* be everything to a man.

"I know," Bret said, his hand covering hers. "Too much, too soon. So I won't say the words I want to say. I won't ask you the question I want to ask."

Charly swallowed, looking down at their entwined hands. "You don't have to . . . you shouldn't, Bret," she said. "I'm a little scared," she admitted awkwardly. "I'm starting to really care about you."

He drew her to him with sudden force, his mouth closing over hers. The all-consuming kiss reverberated with urgency, communicating his need to possess her more eloquently than any words could do. She felt herself melt into his arms, answering that urgency with a fervor of her own, helpless in the surge of wanting, needing him. His kiss swept away all rational thought, leaving her with an overpowering urge for sweet surrender.

"But, damn it, Charly Lynn," he murmured when at last they breathlessly broke apart. "If I *could* do any one thing today, I'll tell you what I'd do!" He held her close to him, and she felt her heart pounding against his. "I'd marry you."

Chapter

8

" 'DEAR MR. HEART: Based on your advice to "Mother Hen" in an earlier column, I gave a man who appealed to me "a chance," and we ended up spending the night. Now he's talking about marriage. Don't you think that a man who's already hearing wedding bells after one night together is a bit suspect? I think I love him, but still I'm tempted to run. What do you think? Yours, Chicken Little.' "

Charly paused to look across the alcove table at Trudy, who nodded thoughtfully and continued cleaning her glasses with a Kleenex.

"And what does Mr. Heart say?"

Charly cleared her throat, smoothed the paper, and continued reading aloud.

" 'Dear Chicken Little: There's nothing suspect about a man who knows what he wants. If it's his sincerity you're questioning, you have two choices: One is to keep seeing him—and see if he means it. The other is to call his bluff now. Say yes! Many successful marriages have resulted from extremely short courtships. So if the feeling is mutual . . . don't forget what they say about gift horses. Yours, Mr. Heart.'"

"A perfectly sensible reply," Trudy said, sparkling glasses now perched on her nose. "Don't you think so, dear?"

Charly put the paper down, drumming her fingers on the tabletop. She had to admit that her levelheaded columnist had a point. "I guess," she agreed uneasily.

"So when are you going out with him again?"

Charly sighed as Trudy fixed her with an expectant look. "After work today."

"Oh, good," Trudy exclaimed, rising from the table. "I'm happy you've come to your senses. Writing Mr. Heart was an excellent idea."

Charly nodded absently as she stared at the dozing parrot above her head. She was excited at the prospect of seeing Bret after a four-day hiatus, yet filled with apprehension. What if they had a wonderful time? What if it was even better than the last time? Although she knew it was crazy to dread the very things that could make her intensely happy, she did.

Immediately following Bret's declaration on the boat, Charly had come down with a serious case of the jitters. Instead of lolling about in bed with him, a lasciviously tempting prospect, she'd hurriedly dressed, making excuses about prior dates in the city, and dragged Harold out of there with all due haste. Bret had been disappointed, but seemed to sense and understand her need for some time alone.

He'd called that night, and the following morning, and the next day . . . and Charly had stalled, ducked, and wriggled out of every invitation he extended. Bret was exasperatingly patient. Why wouldn't he give up on her? And why was she secretly so thrilled that he wouldn't?

"I ought to have my head examined," she grumbled.

"What's that, dear?" Trudy called from the counter.

"Nothing," Charly said. She got up and paced the aisle, ostensibly checking on the health of their ailing gerbils. Time was slowing to a crawl. But it was only a matter of hours before they'd finally be face to face again. She pictured his face, as she had a hundred times since their last good-bye kiss. She replayed that kiss, feeling the same poignant ache of longing... followed by the same tug of fear.

Her letter to Mr. Heart had been meant merely as an exercise, an attempt to sort things out on paper. She hadn't really intended to send it. Finally, as the days away from Bret were nonetheless filled with him, in her mind, she'd mailed the letter. And this morning, after reading Mr. Heart's answer, she'd tossed in the towel. When Bret called, as he'd taken to doing every morning before she left for work, she'd finally agreed to see him.

Those calls! She'd never really understood the erotic capabilities of a phone wire before. Bret would call in the evening, and the sexy sound of his voice was enough to arouse her. But then, when she twisted and turned her way out of his invitations, he would talk about how much he missed her, all the things he wished they were doing together—many of them in specific, intimate detail. By the time she hung up she was usually a quivering mass of unfulfilled desire.

And now, urged on by Trudy and Mr. Heart, she'd given in at last. She had, however, accepted the least threatening of all his invitations: an outdoor barbecue, given by the staff of *S.F.* to celebrate the magazine's tenth year in the business. There'd be lots of people, a kite-flying contest, casual food and drink—it seemed harmless enough. She could meet Bret's friends, spend some time with him, and then leave if she grew uncomfortable. She just wasn't ready for a more intimate tête-à-tête. She wasn't ready for more intimacy, period, although a part of her practically ached at the thought of being in his arms again.

Bret had said she'd be able to find her way to the strip of park near the Presidio by following her nose: the smell of ribs and burgers would be overpowering. Sure enough, after she'd parked in the lot overlooking the marina, Charly easily followed the shoreline near Fort Mason to the hubbub of the *S.F.* cookout.

At first she wandered idly at the edge of the huge lawn, watching the many-colored and variously shaped kites that bobbed in the strong breezes of fresh, salt-scented sea air. In the background, the old-fashioned, sculpted-columned cupola of the Palace of Fine Arts glowed orange in the late afternoon sun.

Charly gazed at the staffers spread out on the grass, along with their friends and families, enjoying the sight of smoke rising in the air from charcoal grills, brightly colored coolers and lawn chairs clustered behind a happily aimless crowd of milling people. She searched the faces, looking for Bret's, feeling her heart beat faster in anticipation of seeing him again, a smile that she couldn't quite control creeping across her face.

It took a few moments before she realized that the lone adult running in dizzying circles amidst a bunch of screaming, laughing kids was the man she'd come to see. Cheered on by his younger companions, Bret was trying, with comic desperation, to coax a Chinese dragon-styled box kite into the air.

Sprinting over the grass in a pair of cut-off khakis and a pale blue button-down shirt, sleeves rolled to the elbow, Bret was barefoot and disheveled. At his side, Smith yelled encouragement, trying to outrun him. The kite wobbled, swooped, rose unsteadily, and then plummeted. Good-natured cheers and laughter greeted this crash-landing. Bret ruefully handed the kite string over to Smith.

"You couldn't get a *balloon* to stay up!" the boy exclaimed, then shrieked happily as Bret took a playful swat at his behind.

"Let's see you do it, then," Bret growled. He looked up, saw Charly for the first time, and waved her over.

Although her pulse was racing, she sauntered toward him at a deliberately slow pace. Bret, however, was making no attempt to mask his excitement at seeing her again; he reached her with a few bounding steps and swept her into his arms.

His warm lips kissed her cheek, then trailed across her soft skin to cover her mouth with a reckless abandon that made her blood pound. Breathless, she clung to him, feeling her heels leave the ground as he pulled her higher and tighter against him.

"Charly, Charly," he cried, swinging her slowly in is enveloping arms. "What's taken you so long?"

"Yuck!" was the exclamation that greeted this public display of affection. Startled, Charly broke from Bret's embrace to find Smith's deep brown eyes narrowed in disapproval.

"Smith," Bret said. "That's no way to greet a lady."

Smith flashed Charly a crooked-toothed grin as she self-consciously smoothed her hair. "Hi, Charly," he said. "Wanna see me make this thing soar like a bird? The chief can't even get it off the ground!"

"I'm ready, Smith," she told him with a smile. The boy gathered up the dragon kite and ran off excitedly. Bret slipped his arm around her waist as they watched him take a jogging start, pulling the kite after him and slowly letting out some string as he ran.

Charly settled into Bret's casual embrace, wondering why it felt so perfectly natural to have this man's arm around her, and why she suddenly felt as if she'd only left his side minutes, not days, ago.

"Way to go, Smith!" Bret called, cupping his mouth with his other hand. The dragon had begun to rise, dipping and turning in its ascent. The young boy beamed at them, running faster as the kite caught the rising wind. "I'm glad you two have hit it off," Bret murmured at her ear.

"He seems like a good kid," Charly said.

Bret nodded, smiling with evident pride at the boy's prowess with the kite. "He is," he said. "He's already accepted you, I can tell. It must have been those cookies." He turned to look at her, his eyes glowing affectionately as he brushed a curl of her windblown hair into place. "He's as rambunctious as Harold. But you seem to have a way with all short fries."

Bret gave her shoulder an affectionate squeeze. Charly managed a wan smile, but her insides were knotting with tension. She knew how much Bret enjoyed being a father to Smith. And she could see that he looked forward to having a son of his own...

The knot tightened. She would have to tell Bret, before long. She wasn't ready to confide in him yet, to share those painful memories and risk the rejection she dreaded. But if he really wanted a future with her, she couldn't be dishonest. Charly swallowed, her throat tight.

"Hungry?"

She looked blankly at Bret. These disturbing thoughts had effectively killed her appetite. "No, not really," she told him. "But don't let me stop you."

She was sure he'd see through her casual phrases and composed features to the underlying pain. Bret was all too adept at sensing her emotional states. But surprisingly, he didn't question her. "I've already had enough ribs to expand my own an inch," he joked, patting his stomach. "But I could go for a glass of wine. How about you?"

Charly nodded as a numbing chill spread through her body. How silly of her, to think that Bret was truly a mind reader, or that he cared enough to question her every word and gesture. Just because they'd spent a night together and he'd said he loved her ... Shouldn't she know better? *Didn't* she know better? Clearly Bret was too caught up in the holiday atmosphere of this gathering of cronies to pay much attention to her.

Even now he was leading her toward a group of people, who were waving and smiling, at a little picnic table. Charly, mentally beginning to step away, disengaging herself from the man at her side, imagined herself as she might be perceived: some woman on Bret Robert's arm, like an attractive appendage. But why, after such a short time spent with him, should she think of herself as more? Because she was more, as they both well knew. Why deny it? Almost angrily, Charly shook her head. She had to, that was why.

Bret was introducing her to a man with a wine bottle in hand. She nodded, smiled, and accepted the drink poured for her, seeing the entire scene as if through the wrong end of a telescope. Only minutes ago she'd felt supremely comfortable with Bret. But now, though she realized she was fueling her own fears, she had the odd sensation of playing a part, faking, going through motions. She didn't know Bret Roberts, really. And he barely knew her.

And she didn't know these people, who were being inordinately friendly, welcoming her without question. An editor, a writer, a photographer—she didn't even try to keep the names straight. They were all congenial, effusive, talking easily with Bret and automatically including her in their conversation. Ordinarily she would have been touched by the way this group of close-knit colleagues were accepting her, the outsider, into their little circle. But now, feeling as alienated as she did, it only made her see them as superficial. They talked so glibly, so smoothly. They would have accepted Bret's date just as quickly if she'd been a nun or a belly dancer. They didn't really care *who* she was.

Charly emptied the rest of her glass and held it out for more wine. She was glad when Bret moved away from her, and the group seemed on the verge of dispersing. Smith came running up to tug on Bret's trousers. Bret gave Charly an apologetic smile, excused himself, and returned to the lawn with the kids and kites. Watching them run off together, Charly felt the knot within her tighten.

With the rush of the wine's warmth, she had a moment of clarity. She realized, intellectually, that she was over-reacting. How could Bret know that the mere sight of him roughhousing with a surrogate son struck fear into her soul? How could she blame him for not understanding things about her he had no way of understanding? But still, the sense of removal stayed with her. She didn't want him to understand, anyway. She'd retreat from this sudden, too-volatile fling as soon as she could. She should have followed her initial instinct.

"Excuse me—you must be Charly."

Charly turned away from the sight of Bret and Smith racing each other across the lawn, grateful for the distraction. The woman facing her had dark hair streaked with gray. She projected the attractive but somewhat harried air of a woman who spent most of her time ensconced in a busy office. Although her eyes were a little bleary and her complexion pale, Charly recognized the keen look of an always-engaged intellect in her expression.

"I'm Harriet Lowe, the managing editor," she said, extending her hand with a friendly smile. "Welcome to the *S.F.* zoo." She was pointing to a tumultuous group starting up an impromptu frisbee throw a few yards off.

Charly smiled. "Thanks," she said. "They seem like a nice group of guys."

"Oh, sure," Harriet agreed, lighting up a cigarette. "Just a little obstreperous when it comes to feeding time." She threw her match away, observing Charly through a cloud of smoke. "So, you're the one," she mused.

"The one what?" Charly asked apprehensively.

"The one who's got Bret Roberts three feet off the ground," Harriet replied with a throaty chuckle. "Not what I expected. Better," she added quickly, as Charly looked at her, startled. "Gorgeous—but you look like you've got a head on your shoulders."

Charly cleared her throat. "Has Bret been dating headless women?"

Harriet laughed. "No, and I'm sorry. I shouldn't be talking to you like this. Roberts would kill me. I only meant that from the way he's been flying around and the few things he's said, I expected a sorceress to float in on a cloud of frankincense, reeking of aphrodisiacal perfumes."

Charly raised her eyebrows at the woman's hyperbole. "I'm from Massachusetts," she said wryly. "Why, what's he been saying?"

Harriet smiled, shaking her head. "Oh, no, I'm not going to get myself in any hot water. But you've certainly turned his head around."

They both gazed out at the lawn, where Bret was now hoisting Smith up on his shoulders, the boy excitedly holding his spool of string aloft. After a moment Charly turned back to Harriet. "I haven't known Bret too long, actually," she said.

Harriet nodded. "I guess it's a case of love at first sight," she sighed. "I wouldn't know about such things. Oh, I mean, *his* first sight," she added at Charly's wary look. "How many feet do I have in my mouth now?"

Charly smiled, enjoying the woman and her tobacco-hoarse voice. A new feeling of well-being was replacing her earlier discomfort. "None," she assured Harriet. "It's nice to hear I made an impression."

"An impression?" Harriet scoffed. "Changed his life is more like it. Well, I'm glad he's finally going to do what he's been wanting to do. Though we'll miss him."

That newly gained well-being began evaporating rapidly. "Miss him?" she said. "He's leaving *S.F.?*"

Harriet winced, a look of pure chagrin on her face. "Whoops," she muttered. "I think I've now said every conceivable thing I wasn't supposed to say. Maybe I'd better trundle along."

"No, that's all right," Charly said quickly. "I haven't seen Bret in a few days. We haven't had a chance to catch up on things."

"If I've spoiled any surprises Bret was going to spring, he'll throttle me," Harriet said worriedly. "I'm really sorry. But he's been so excited. I just assumed..."

"Don't worry," Charly said, although she was already wondering how many more surprises this reunion with Bret was going to yield. "Is he going through with his plans for a paper of his own?" she ventured, remembering their conversation on the houseboat.

Harriet's features relaxed into a smile. "That's right," she said. "But I'm sure he'll fill you in on all the details. Look, I left a hamburger on the fire over there, so I'd better go see if it's burnt to a crisp or already on someone else's bun." She held her hand out again. "I'm glad we met."

"Yes, it was good to meet you," Charly said, shaking her hand.

"I have a good feeling about you," Harriet said with a sudden vehemence that Charly found endearing. "Any woman named Charly's okay in my book. You're probably better than what that rascal Roberts deserves, but..." She gave a philosophical shrug, then winked. "I bet you'll straighten him out. See you."

"Thanks, Harriet. So long." Feeling somewhat dazed,

Charly watched the woman vanish into a cluster of people around one of the grills. Her emotions were a churning mass of confused fears, doubts, annoyances, and skewed hopes. Did she know Bret Roberts at all?

Here he was now, striding toward her, his hair unkempt, knees grass-stained, beaming at her in the last rays of the setting sun. Without a word he pulled her to him, brushing his lips across hers in a teasingly light kiss of greeting. Charly responded without thinking, her lips parting to receive his, her body seeming to melt into his strong, warm embrace with a will of its own. In the brief moment of their kiss it seemed as if the world and all her inner tumult disappeared.

She drank in the sweetness of his mouth, the feel of him against her that was oddly familiar, the scent of him that already conjured up erotic memories. But then their lips parted, and she was staring into the soft blue eyes as though they were a stranger's, barely knowing who it was she'd just clung to so urgently.

"What's wrong?" he asked, his eyes narrowing.

"Nothing," she said, looking away, but he captured her chin with his thumb and forefinger.

"You're angry that I've abandoned you."

"No," she said. "I'm fine."

"Sure," he said, frowning. "And I'm an Eskimo. Talk to me, Charly."

Now you're noticing, she thought ruefully. Where were you when I began to spin out a while ago? "There's nothing to talk about," she said in a careless tone. "Should we get more wine?"

"No." He gazed at her thoughtfully. "I think we should take a walk."

Charly shrugged. "If you like. Think Smith will mind?"

She'd meant the remark facetiously, but Bret paused, examining her more closely. "No, he can take care of himself," he said slowly. "But are you minding? Charly, you're not annoyed that I've been off flying a kite with the kid, are you?"

"Of course not," she said quickly.

"I didn't think so," he said, taking her arm. "And I'm glad. You see, I try to spend as much time with Smith as I can on a weekend like this—all of us guys do." He shook his head, brow creased. "I guess I know more than any of them what it's like to be without a father. Mine was alive, of course, but he was never really there."

Charly was silent, her throat tightening as he spoke. She could sense, with mounting dread, the direction his thoughts were taking.

"So I try to make the kid feel special, feel wanted. I pay attention to what he does, even if it's geting into trouble." He smiled grimly. "I miss the closeness I could have had with my dad. I've tried to make Smith feel it. And I sure hope I can make it happen when I've got a kid of my own."

Charly blanched, the sound of his earnest wish like a bell tolling death to her own hopes. She looked away, trying to disguise the swell of stricken feelings that rose within her. Fortunately, Bret was gazing off down the shoreline when she stole a look at him.

"Sorry," he said, when his eyes met hers again. "I didn't mean to pontificate. And I guess I left you high and dry over there. I hope you weren't bored out of your mind with all these magazine people."

"Not in the least," she assured him, glad to change the subject. "I've been enjoying myself, talking to some of your friends here."

"Which ones?" he asked, as they began ambling toward the edge of the picnic area. "Someone telling you about my disreputable past, no doubt . . . Charly, something's on your mind."

Charly shook her head. They were approaching the path that followed the shoreline toward the marina, heading away from the hubbub of the barbecue crowd. Already the bay was on fire with the last rays of the sun's descent. "I met Harriet Lowe," she said.

"Uh-oh," Bret muttered. "Harriet the Mouth. I love that woman," he added, "but she does tend to talk. Okay, Charly, what horrible pieces of my darkest past has she been dredging up for you?"

Charly smiled thinly. "None whatsoever. But she did tell me something about your future that gave me pause."

Bret stopped abruptly, turning to face Charly. Overhead, seagulls cawed, flapping away from them in the purpling sky. "She spilled the beans, didn't she?" he said ruefully. "About my new plan of action?"

"She said you were leaving the magazine."

He nodded. "I'm going off the masthead over at *Omnibus* as well, and all the other periodicals and papers. Did she tell you why?"

"No," Charly admitted. "But I think I figured it out. You're going to start a paper of your own, just like you were talking about."

"Like *we* were talking about," he corrected her. "In fact, I owe this speedy turn of events to you."

"Me?" She stared at him, startled.

"Yes, you," he said, leaning forward to brush his lips gently across her forehead. His eyes sparkled as he tenderly caressed her cheek with his fingers with a shiver-provoking stroke. "I've been wanting to do this for the longest time, but it wasn't until I talked about my idea with you that I decided to take the plunge," he said with a sheepish grin.

Charly stared at him, wondering, but thrilled at the feel of his warm skin against hers and the excited look in his eyes. "You listened to me," he went on quietly. "And you questioned me, and you made me follow through on all the thoughts I had about it. I could feel your faith in the idea, your faith in me." He smiled. "It made a difference. *You've* made a difference, to say the least, Charly. I've decided it's time to take some risks, maybe because I've found something—someone—worth taking risks for."

Charly swallowed. "This sounds wonderful, Bret," she said. "But it wasn't me. You're the one who—"

"It's you," he broke in, kissing her chin, lifting her face up to his. "Things started falling into place the moment we met. I had a feeling then, and it keeps growing stronger. I've started thinking about a future, a real future, for the first time."

Charly looked away from his incandescent gaze, more torn and uncertain than ever. She had a feeling that he thought his future included her, and that thought gave her such foreboding . . .

"What we should do is celebrate, you and I," Bret said, his fingers gently stroking her cheek. The light caress made her skin tingle, inflamed her blood with erotic memory. Looking into his eyes again, it was hard to get her bearings, to pull away. His excitement was contagious; it overpowered her lingering doubts and fears.

"What did you have in mind?" she asked warily. She knew that if she didn't break away from him immediately, she'd end up in his arms. But was that such a terrible prospect? His caresses could drive all doubts away. She knew she wanted to relive the passion she'd enjoyed so intensely.

"A drink," he said with a mischievous smile.

Charly sighed. Resistance seemed ridiculous. "Well . . ."

"Just one," he suggested, eyes twinkling.

"Just one," she agreed.

Chapter

9

"KIDNAPPED AGAIN!" SHE moaned as Bret escorted her through the polished darkwood door.

"That's right," he said, closing it behind her.

Charly sighed, looking around the luxurious hotel suite. Through a large picture window at the far end of the carpeted room, the lights of San Francisco twinkled brightly. Through another doorway, she could glimpse a sumptuous canopied bed.

"Bret," she said, turning to look at him in the semi-darkness. "This is not what I call going out for a drink."

"We're ordering in," he said nonchalantly. "I already alerted room service when we arrived."

Charly shook her head. Things weren't going at all as she'd planned. Spirited to this hotel atop Nob Hill in Bret's jeep, she'd reluctantly agreed to a drink in the establishment's top floor bar. Only when Bret made an abrupt turn, produced a room key, and hustled her down the hall to this beautifully appointed room had she realized there was no escaping. And now, even as she opened her mouth to protest again, Bret's lips silenced hers with a devastating kiss.

It took too much effort to resist. She returned the kiss with a fervor that matched his, realizing dumbly that being deprived of Bret's kisses had only made her desire them more. Her hands slid around his neck as he pulled her closer to him, and she succumbed to the pounding heat that his eager tongue elicited, rising flamelike within her core.

"Charly," he murmured breathlessly, his lips only inches from hers as she arched her back, leaning into the cradling embrace of his arms. "I've been feeling you pull away from me all day, all night. Why, love? What's changed between us?"

At the moment, she couldn't answer. When he held her like this, the fears she'd felt before faded, rendered insignificant by her overwhelming desire to merge with him again—as if pure physical abandon would make everything all right. But Bret's eyes held a challenge, and a commanding stubborn gleam that told her it was useless to avoid talking any longer.

"Nothing," she murmured. "And everything..."

"Come with me." He released her from his sheltering embrace and took her by the hand. Stiffening in nervous anticipation, she let him lead her to the couch by the picture window. Gently but firmly, he pulled her down to sit facing him, the city lights glowing behind them.

"Okay," he said quietly. "It's honesty time. For the next few minutes, all evasions, white lies, avoidances of issues, and unspoken thoughts are absolutely taboo, banned, and outlawed. Shake on it." And he held out his hand.

Charly couldn't help but smile at his grave expression

and his formally extended hand. Nonetheless, she dutifully shook on the deal, then leaned back against the soft plushness of the couch. A pulse thudded loudly in her ears as he studied her face.

"You've been avoiding me since you left my boat last Saturday," he said evenly. "And if you could have managed it, you wouldn't have spent a minute alone with me tonight. Why?"

Charly stared at him, took a deep breath, and then exhaled. "I've been . . . worried," she said carefully.

"You mean scared," he corrected. "It was stupid of me to say that terrifying word, *marriage*," he went on with an ironic smile. "It was much too soon, and I can't blame you for thinking I might be just a little bit loony."

Charly shifted uneasily in her seat. "I know you're not . . . loony," she began. "But things have been happening so quickly."

"I blurted out what I felt," he said, frowning. "And I still feel that way," he added, rubbing his cheek thoughtfully with his palm. "I happen to think that when lightning strikes, you know it. And I know, deep in my gut, that there's only one person in the world I want to be with from now on: you."

Charly looked into his loving gaze and felt a tremor of excitement ripple through her. No man had ever said such words to her, so simply and so meaningfully—not even the man she'd married. But even as she looked into those sweetly glowing azure eyes, she felt the fear hovering around her heart. "But Bret," she said, "there are so many things we don't know about each other."

"Ask my anything you want to know," he offered. "I'll be an open book. Tell me anything you want to tell me. I know you've been married once; but that was obviously to the wrong man, so I can't hold it against you," he added, smiling. "But Charly, we don't have to talk about the future if the future makes you nervous.

I'm willing to wait for you, as long as it may take. I just want you to know I'm serious. I don't throw proposals around lightly. In fact, I've never even *thought* about a commitment like that before—it was always some distant fantasy."

"I guess I do need some time," Charly said. "I loved being with you last weekend," she admitted softly. "Maybe I need time to assure myself that there's more to us than . . ."

"More than the most fantastic lovemaking?" he said, and shook his head, his hand closing over hers again. "I know there is. This isn't just a physical thing, Charly. You've inspired me to take a giant step forward. My life's changing already. I'm only wondering what it is that I can do for you—to give you back what you've already given me."

The soft pulse beating beneath his hand quickened as she gazed into his eyes. Love surged through her. How could she explain that he was giving her so much, even now? She'd almost stopped believing that another human being—another man—could care for her as she might care for him. She'd been bitter, and distrustful, convinced that all a man could think about was himself, that she could never share the things she wanted to share, to be understood the way she needed to be understood. And now this man was showing her, with the softest words and subtlest gestures, that she'd been wrong.

"You're doing a good job," she murmured, bringing his hand to her lips. He smiled as she tenderly brushed the warm skin with her mouth.

"Am I?"

She nodded, feeling a poignant tug within her at his trusting look. She wanted to tell him about her secret fears. She wanted to tell him about the pain she'd felt, and the painful uncertainty that still lingered. What would he say if she told him that a future for them might be horribly incomplete. That it might be childless.

She couldn't. Not yet. She couldn't bear the thought of her new found happiness being torn away in a single stroke. "Hold me," she cried suddenly, wanting only to lose herself in wordless affirmation of their love. "Oh, Bret, just hold me, now . . ."

He pulled her close, his lips seeking hers. "Darling," he murmured.

A soft knock on the door interrupted them. Bret let go of her only long enough to flick the light switch on behind him. A soft rosy glow illuminated the foyer. "Come in," he called.

The hotel clerk, eyes averted, wheeled a tray into the room and was gone before Charly had a chance to feel embarrassed, caught as she was imprisoned in Bret's arms.

"Drinks?" she asked.

Bret's eyes held hers. "I'm already too intoxicated," he confessed, bringing his lips to hers again.

Their kiss was fevered. Lips melded, tongues searched for a taste of the other as if both were truly starved. His hands roved her body, drawing her to him, taking possession of every line and curve with a loving caress. Lips still pressed tightly in a deepening kiss, he began to lead her toward the bedroom.

It became a game, prolonging the kiss, moving together as one with the bed an inexorable destination. She felt a laugh of delight bubble up within her, and an answering smile in his pursed lips, as they moved slowly across the plushly carpeted floor.

When at last the bed was within reach, Charly kicked off her shoes, as did Bret, and then, with a deep-throated laugh, he pulled her to him. They tumbled down upon the covers. Now it was she who took the lead, pushing him onto his back, her hands eager to grasp at buttons, to push the shirt from his trousers, to feel the curly tendrils of his chest hair beneath her restlessly moving fingers.

She loved the way his breath caught and quickened, the way he willingly let her push the shirt from his shoulders, a moan escaping his half-open lips as she knelt to kiss his taut abdomen. Then, with a growl, he pulled her closer, his rough-velvet tongue parting her lips, his gentle hands unbuttoning her dress.

Her body was tingling with anticipation as he pulled the material past her shoulders, his eyes drinking in the sight of her trembling flesh as she straddled him on the bed. He ran his hands over the lush contours of her breasts, gently fondling the taut pink tips until her breath came deep and ragged.

There was a frenzy of clothing pushed and pulled, discarded in haste. She wanted to feel the fullness of his naked body next to hers, and she tugged at his recalcitrant belt until, chuckling softly in the darkness, he helped her with it. Silently they undressed each other, kisses and caresses the only interruptions of their urgent disrobing.

When at last they were naked, skin to skin, they slowed again. His hands played lightly across her body, lingering to explore the undercurve of her breasts, the hollow of her waist, her rounded thighs and the shadowy valley between them. Charly's arms opened wide to enfold him, her own hands molding themselves to his buttocks, fitting his hips possessively to hers.

The silky friction of flesh against flesh and the moist gliding of their lips as their hearts raced in unison was soon too much to savor slowly. Their limbs entwined suddenly, and they strained to be even closer, smiling, kissing, and touching with the delighted abandon of two children.

But there wasn't anything childlike about the strong masculine body pressed against hers. She ran her palms over his shoulders and the sinewy muscles of his back, the gentle rasp of his stubbly chin against her breasts exciting her beyond endurance. His hands were demanding and persuasive, coaxing her nipples to tender aching points, bringing her to the brink of moist, trembling arousal.

Their mutual desire was escalating, the dark room filling with the sound of their ragged breathing and the twisting and turning on the deep soft bed. In a whisper that was husky with passion he told her of his love, told her how she felt against him, told her what he wanted as he parted her legs, poised above her, waiting for her to answer him in kind. Body taut, she arched herself upward, taking him inside her as he thrust, groaning, her embrace a silent welcome.

Soon she was writhing feverishly beneath him, wrapping her legs around his waist as he enfolded her with his powerful body, whispering endearments. With intoxicating kisses and wild, then tender, touches, he urged her forward, onward into ecstasy.

"Charly," he breathed. "Open your eyes."

She looked at him, seeing each quake and shiver of pleasure reflected in his smoldering gaze, and something more. "Yes," she murmured.

"Love, don't look away."

"Yes, Bret." Her voice was a husky moan.

"My love," he gasped.

And then she gazed into his eyes, and their rhythm mounted as the feeling inside of her swelled to a spiraling, bursting peak. She cried his name aloud, and he, hers. Bodies thrashing, thrusting, melding at last into one white-hot nova of delirious release, she watched him watching her, saw herself in his eyes, saw her own exultation shining, merged with his. They reached the pinnacle together, gazes locked in breathless wonder, and then at last, he kissed her lips again, and she fell back into sweet and blissful darkness.

Floating in the dark, his body sprawled beside hers,

Charly moved with a sigh of contentment to fit her body to his, already slipping into sleep. It was only then, as her consciousness hovered between dreaming and wakefulness, that the image glimmered faintly in her mind: Bret, lithe and manly, running joyously over green grass in the orange sun-glow . . . and beside him, a child, tightly clutching a kite string. She saw the small boy's hand in Bret's and the happiness in his eyes, as she tossed and turned, fitfully, drifting into troubled sleep.

Dear Mr. Heart:
I'm writing again. Thanks! Your advice was terrific, but now I must ask for your help on another matter:

Charly's pen hovered over the lined paper. She wanted to be candid, straightforward. No beating around the bush, she told herself grimly, glancing at her first two drafts, crumpled on the desk beside her.

But it wasn't easy. She knew that Mr. Heart's sensitivity and understanding knew no bounds. That was the reason she was seeking his advice before talking to Bret. Still, the idea of seeing her most intimate problem printed in the newspaper was suddenly intimidating.

She had to do it, though. Keeping this secret was beginning to drive her crazy. Thoughts of all she had withheld from Bret hovered like a cloud about to cover the sun, whenever she spoke to him. And she spoke to him every night.

Soon, she would see him face to face. She was suddenly glad he'd been out of town most of the week. He was now in Los Angeles, finalizing arrangements to get his paper started. He hadn't given her many details, not wanting to jinx the deal until he was sure everything would go through.

But about all else, he was effusively open. He was running up what had to be an enormous phone bill, sometimes staying on the line for hours as they shared stories, reminiscences, intimate details of their lives. In her attempt to be as open as he, Charly was revealing things about her past that she hadn't thought of in years, tales of high-school romances, for example.

But she still hadn't mentioned her miscarriages. In fact, she'd avoided the whole painful subject of her marriage, although she knew she'd have to tell him eventually. So now, before she saw him again, she wanted a chance to get some coaching and some insight from the man who'd been so helpful before.

Brow creased in concentration, Charly began to write again. She outlined the problem in black and white, explaining her worries about disappointing the man who claimed he loved her and wanted to create a future with her. And when she was done with this draft, she felt a relief that was overwhelming. It felt good just to put it all down on paper.

After much inward debate, she decided to mark the letter "Confidential." That was the best approach, she decided. Mr. Heart wouldn't print her letter, but he would print a reply. In this way she'd be spared the embarrassment of seeing her own words in the *Sun*.

She found an envelope, stamped and addressed it. And then, though it was already evening, she walked down to the corner mailbox. She didn't want to wait a minute longer than necessary to get a reply. Bret was a sensitive and understanding man, but there was no telling how he would react to the knowledge that Charly might never have children. Mr. Heart, on the other hand, was bound to put everything into the right perspective. Maybe he would suggest a way to break it to Bret gently, or at least give her the necessary courage for the inevitable.

In any event, she was sure he'd have something helpful to say. He hadn't let her down so far, had he? Feeling better about the whole situation for the first time in days, Charly dropped her letter into the slot. She hummed to herself as she walked back home to await Bret's call.

Chapter

10

"IT'S A LOT nicer in daylight," Charly said as, arm in arm with Bret, she turned down Bridgeway, the main street of Sausalito. She hadn't been able to get even a sense of the town the last time she'd been here. But now, under a sunny blue sky, she could see why the community was such a popular tourist attraction.

The scenery alone was spectacular: steep hills topped with white and beige houses, a glittering forest of ship's masts bobbing on the bay below, and the San Francisco skyline gleaming in the distance. Though she'd never been to the French Riviera, this blend of the swank and bohemian restaurants and shops put her in mind of pictures she'd seen of those European resorts.

"It's also less crowded during the week," Bret said, as they sidestepped a slow-moving gaggle of sun-visored tourists.

"Oh, I don't mind the crowd," she told him. Bret smiled, guiding her along the sidewalk, which was lined with art galleries and boutiques.

"I'm assuming you mean you only have eyes for me," he joked.

"Uh-uh," she informed him solemnly. "I only have eyes for that amazing jewelry over there." She was pointing to a display of sparking handmade necklaces that hung in the window behind him. "Let's take a look."

She smiled as he groaned in mock-exasperation at her penchant for window-shopping. Within this first hour of her arrival by ferry, she'd already scoured at least a dozen of the Sausalito stores and galleries. Bret had indulged her while keeping a smug smile on his face when she asked about his Los Angeles trip.

But within another block or two, she was ready to sit down and eager to have a more lengthy talk. Not that she felt she had very much to catch up on. Bret's nightly phone calls had kept them each well-informed of the other's comings and goings during this week of separation, from Bret's favorite Hollywood taco tales to Charly's misadventures with a runaway hamster in The Sanctuary.

She was ready for intimate talk, though, and more intimate contact than his light, shiver-inducing caresses on her arms and shoulders as they walked down the boulevard. Thoughts of the night ahead—she'd brought a change of clothes in her bag, as it was tacitly understood she would stay the weekend—gave this leisurely afternoon walk a delicious anticipatory undertone.

"Here's a good spot," Bret announced, steering her into an oak-paneled tavern right off the street. He guided her through the dark and cozy bar to a sunlit garden in the rear, where people at various tables were engaged in games of checkers, chess, and Scrabble, or just good, spirited conversation. The sounds of soft, low-key jazz floated across the little courtyard as they took their seats in one corner.

"This is nice," she said, looking around her. "What's it called?"

"It isn't," Bret said. "This is the bar with no name. Apparently the original owners could never agree on what to call it."

Charly smiled. The idea somehow made perfect sense as she surveyed the homey place. Bret waved hello to a deeply sunburnt man in a skipper's hat who was smoking a pipe, paperback in hand, at the opposite corner. "That's the fellow who gave us a tow into the dock," Bret told her.

Charly nodded. A waitress appeared, and Bret convinced Charly to try the house special, an exotic-looking drink made of gin, various fruits, curacao, and cream.

"Now," Charly commanded. "Let's hear it. Are you about to create the *Bret Roberts Times?*"

Bret chuckled. "Not quite. But I've got a paper, all right: the North Beach *Voice.*"

"Really? But that's fantastic, Bret. How did you manage it?"

His grin broadened at her incredulous stare. "I happen to know the man who was about to buy it. He was planning to merge it with the *Herald* as a sort of *National Enquirer*-type sensational weekly," he said. "I made him an interesting offer."

"Wait a second," Charly said, the light beginning to dawn. "Isn't the *Herald* one of—"

"My grandfather's papers, yes."

"You bought the *Voice* from your grandfather?"

"My grandfather owns it, my dad manages it, but I'm going to run it—as the new editor."

The enormity of his accomplishment suddenly hit her. "You mean... you've gone into business with your father?"

Bret nodded, seeming to savor the irony of the situation. His eyes gleamed with amusement at Charly's surprise. When the drinks arrived, he held his glass aloft and said, "To the beginning of a new era—and a new life."

Charly clinked her glass to his, then sipped the delicious mixture, which went down her throat like spiced velvet. "You'd better explain the details," she said.

"It's actually quite simple." Bret covered her hand with his own, eyes alight with excitement. "I'd already had a conversation with my dad about it over the phone. But he didn't take me seriously until I showed up at his office and pitched my idea, with the demographics to back me up. The *Voice* had been losing circulation since Burstein, the original publisher, died a year or so ago; they'd been losing their focus and their readers. My dad's solution, typically, was to turn it into a tabloid rag." Bret paused, sipped his drink, then went on:

"I told him I wanted to take it over and breathe some life into it, make it a great weekly paper again—my way. I promised him I'd up the circulation within a year—or let him take control again. In the meantime, though, he'd have to let me do as I wanted—hands off, on his end. I'd only do business with him on my terms."

"And he accepted?"

"The prodigal son, coming back into the fold? How could he resist?" Bret grinned. "But he's biting the bullet, and he knows it. He knows I'm going to prove to him— and San Francisco—that you can sell a paper on the basis of good, solid journalism instead of exploitation and sensational filler. So I haven't compromised. I've just begun to achieve a lifelong ambition"—he squeezed her hand—"with your help."

"Bret, this was all your idea," she demurred, though a warm thrill went through her at his meaningful caress. "I just happened to be there when you talked about it."

"That's right," he said wryly. "You just happened to be there. And I want you to keep right on just happening to be here. Because, don't you see, Charly? I'm doing this for us."

"How do you mean?"

His eyes held hers with a look of admiration. "Darling, I'm tired of stretching myself over six different offices, working here and there, running around. I'm ready to settle down, in one place, with one woman. And you're it, Charly."

She stared at him, taken aback by the certainty in his voice. So he wanted to settle down. Charly knew full well what a phrase like that implied.

"I hope that worried look in your eye doesn't mean doubt about this plan," Bret said. "It's going to work."

"Of course it will," she said quickly. "Congratulations, Bret. I just know you'll be successful."

"I was hoping for more than a hearty handshake," he murmured. "Don't worry, no one will arrest us."

With a sheepish smile, Charly brought her lips to meet his. The kiss was sweet and gentle, yet to her it had a sting. Even as she savored the warm, moist feel of his mouth claiming hers, she felt a twinge of guilt. Since their conversation in the hotel a week earlier, he hadn't said another word about marriage. There was a tacit understanding that they'd approach that subject when the time felt right.

But now Bret seemed to be proceeding as if their future together weren't in question. And why should he think otherwise? she mused as they ended their kiss. She sat back, instinctively running her tongue over her lips, and smiled, self-conscious, as his eyes lingered on her lips, with a mischievous glint.

"You know, there is actually some champagne back at my boat," Bret said. "If we wanted to celebrate a little more before dinner..."

"I see," Charly said, picking up on the subtly erotic undertone in his casual offer. "You mean, a more private celebration?"

"Exactly," he murmured. "Interested?"

"I might be," she said, trying to match his carelessly flirtatious tone. But her mind and emotions were in turmoil. Even as he signaled the waitress for their check, his hand still covering hers, she couldn't stop turning a decision over and over again in her mind.

Mr. Heart had yet to print a reply to her confidential letter. How long would it take? She didn't think she could live with her doubts and fears for one more night. She'd have to tell Bret soon, have to find out if her hopes for happiness with him were destined to die. She couldn't wait for the columnist's advice.

As they walked from the no-name bar back out to Bridgeway, strolling toward the docks, she wondered how she could ever broach the subject: *By the way, Bret, I know you're interested in settling down with me, but I think you should know we might not be raising a family . . .*

The very thought brought a chill to her bones. But she'd have to talk about it, somehow, and soon. Tonight. If they were going to spend any more time together, if she was going to fall any deeper in love with him, she'd have to be honest with this man. How could a relationship like theirs go on without total trust?

"You're awfully thoughtful, Charly."

His husky voice at her ear brought her back to the present moment, and Charly smiled at him. "Sorry," she said. "Just meditating about . . . the future."

He nodded. "There's a lot to think about. We've got a lot to talk about too, Charly. There are a few things I've been meaning to tell you."

"Oh?" She suppressed an inner shudder. "Well, there's something I'd like to talk to you about, too, Bret."

He nodded, as if lost in his own thoughts, then quickly changed the subject. As they wended their way down to the docks, he pointed out the various sights of Sausalito to her. She tried to enjoy the afternoon sun's play on the sparkling bay water, to lose herself in the comforting, secure feeling of Bret's arm around her.

There was the boat, its nondescript exterior giving no clue to the more luxurious environment within. Bret helped her on board, then leaned over the side, inspecting a rope that was trailing into the water. "I've got some champagne chilling," he explained, slowly pulling the rope up. She watched him hoist a bucket onto the railing and check the bottles glistening in it. "Maybe a few more minutes," he decided, then lowered the bucket again. "Go on in."

Charly stepped through the doors into the main cabin. Everything was as she'd remembered it, with one glaring exception: Bret's office area looked as if a small tornado had run through it. Piles of papers lay scattered across the desktop, pulled files spilled over each other on the floor. Bret was obviously in the middle of some massive work-oriented housecleaning.

"I'm trying to tie up loose ends at all the magazines and papers," he said, coming in behind her. "Clearing the decks before I start in over at the *Voice.*"

Charly nodded, taking a seat in a chair by the window. Bret leaned over to plant a gentle kiss on her forehead before kneeling down in front of her seat.

"I'll probably be working around the clock at first," he told her quietly. "And I won't be able to see you as much as I'd like."

Was that what he wanted to discuss with her? Charly met his solemn gaze with an encouraging smile. "That's all right, Bret," she said. "I know you'll have your hands full for a while."

"I'd like to have my hands full of you and nothing

more," he said, sliding his hands around her neck and easing her face forward so he could kiss, in quick succession, her eyelids, nose, and chin. Charly closed her eyes, reveling in the gentle brush of his lips.

"But I'll make time for us to be together," he went on, his fingers playing with the curls at the back of her neck. "I'm even considering getting another place in the city, so I won't have to commute."

"That would be good," she said, flushing slightly as he tickled the outlines of her ears, his smile widening at her words.

"You wouldn't mind me living closer to you, then?"

"Not that much." She smiled at the seriousness of his gaze.

"Charly, I want you to be . . . open to things, to all sorts of possibilities," he said slowly. "You never know what the future could bring us, how things might work out."

She looked at him, a bit disconcerted. She wasn't sure what he was getting at. "I haven't the slightest idea how things will work out," she told him truthfully. "But what do you mean?"

"I mean . . ." He frowned, brow furrowed in concentration. "There are some things I haven't been able to share with you, up until now. But the time has come to clear the air. I want you to be able to trust me, Charly, as I'm already trusting you."

She stared at him mutely, that tug of poignant bitterness pulling at her insides again. He was worried about her trust in him? It was an ironic thing for him to worry about, when she was only now preparing to be fully honest with him, herself.

"I do trust you, Bret," she said softly, putting a hand on his shoulder. "I'm not afraid to share things with you anymore. You've taught me a little bit about being honest, and I . . . I'm the one who should be worried. There's still a lot about me you don't know."

"No, Charly." He shook his head, an oddly pained expression on his face. "Don't worry. Nothing you could tell me would change anything." Then he looked away, gazing moodily at the desk and its piles of strewn paper. "I just hope..." Bret's voice trailed off, and he stood abruptly. "I'll get that champagne," he said. "Then we can settle down for a real heart-to-heart."

Charly looked up at him, wondering if the man was prescient. Was he so sensitive that he could tell she needed some time to gather her strength, that she was about to confront something that could be truly painful? "Okay," she said. "I'll be right here."

He looked at her a moment, his expression unfathomable, then turned and left the cabin. Charly sighed and stood up, restlessly pacing. How had things gotten serious so fast? Shaking her head, she wandered over to the desk, idly glancing through the seemingly random piles.

There were clippings from *Omnibus,* a stack of *Sporting News*... Catching sight of an unfamiliar logo, she leaned over and lifted a pile of press clippings. Unfortunately, her elbow caught on an adjacent stack of newspapers, and the entire bunch slid from the desktop to the floor.

With an exclamation of dismay, Charly knelt down beneath the desk, hurriedly gathering the papers into as orderly a pile as she could manage. Some had fluttered out of reach, one covering a carton shoved between the desk and wall. On her hands and knees, she stretched to grab it, then froze suddenly as she saw what was inside the carton.

The black silhouette in a white heart was unmistakable, an instantly recognizable insignia. Her heart thudding thunderously in her ears, Charly reached over, and pulled the carton closer. It was filled with stationery—

with Mr. Heart's name embossed on top.

What in God's name was Bret Roberts doing with a box of stationery emblazoned with her columnist's logo? Eyes widening in disbelief, she gazed at the clearly masculine script covering the top sheet. Was Mr. Heart a friend of Bret's? Good Lord, did the man share his mail with other journalists, or ... ?

Her fingers trembled as she scanned the writing, then turned the sheet over. Paper-clipped to the back was a handwritten letter in a feminine script. She felt she had suddenly stumbled into the middle of some Twilight Zone nightmare. These were Mr. Heart's letters, with his replies, all in a neat file.

Pulse pounding, throat dry, she gaped at the date neatly penciled in on the topmost letter. The 22nd, this past Thursday!

The realization hit her, as fast and toppling as a sudden fist jammed into her stomach. He'd read them. He'd read all the letters: Trudy's first one, her second, and ...

No. It couldn't be.

But it had to be.

She wasn't sure she could even stand up. She'd never experienced vertigo while kneeling on the floor, but that was the nauseated feeling she suffered as she slowly rose, the letter clutched in her hand.

"Charly!"

Bret was standing frozen in the doorway, a dripping champagne bottle in each of his fists. His eyes, guilt-stricken as they met hers, revealed everything, confirmed each nightmarish fear.

"Charly," he began, moving forward. "I was about to tell you. I was going to explain, to ..."

If he said anything more, she never heard it. She was running, blood pounding, brushing past him and out the door. She kept running, even as the angry tears of humiliation started coursing down her cheeks, and she couldn't quite see where she was going.

He knew! Everything she'd been so frightened of telling him—he knew it all! What did he think? What would happen now?

And why should she care? Charly thought, as mortification gave way to a jolt of pure rage. As far as she could tell, there was no reason for her to ever see that lying, two-faced louse again!

Chapter

11

"I DON'T WANT to hear it."

"But, Charly—"

"No way."

"Charly, it's his farewell column."

"That's just dandy."

Trudy sighed, gazing at Charly across the little table in The Sanctuary's alcove. "He's written to someone called 'Confidential,' you know."

Charly stared at Trudy, lips set tight. "So?"

"So, don't you want to hear what he has to say?"

"What makes you think I'm interested?" Charly snapped, scowling at the myna bird before it even opened its beak. "I'll feed you in a minute."

"Just a hunch," Trudy said mildly.

"Ha!" Charly cried, with a vehemence that sent the bird scurrying to another corner of its cage, feathers ruffling. "You mean after I've been unscrupulously manipulated and betrayed by a deviously deceitful person, I should still be interested in what he has to say?"

Trudy sighed again, folding the newspaper. "He's apologizing to you. In print."

"He can do it in skywriting for all I care," Charly spat. "That man is the lowest."

"I don't think so," Trudy said, indignant. "Why, think of all the people he's helped with this column! He can't be as bad as you're painting him to be." She frowned, patting the paper. "I'll miss him, and I bet half of San Francisco will miss him, too."

"Minus one," Charly reminded her.

"You already do," Trudy muttered. "You miss him."

"Never."

"You haven't been the same since last weekend," Trudy said, her knowing look magnified by a tilt of her bifocals. "Charly, I've never seen you so seriously depressed."

"If I am depressed," Charly said slowly, "it's because I'm disappointed. That skunk nearly had me believing there was hope for mankind, and hope for this woman who was fool enough to trust a man. I should have known better."

"He's in love with you," Trudy stated simply, with the quiet authority of one playing a trump card.

"Tough luck," Charly said.

"And you're in love with him," she continued calmly. "It's just like in the beginning: the lady doth protest—"

"Careful," Charly said in a withering tone. "I'd rather not dwell on who was actually responsible for bringing my plight to Mr. Heart's attention in the first place."

Trudy cleared her throat, rising from the table. "Well, I guess I should see how our new hamster is faring," she said. She stood by the table, briefly toying with the edge of the newspaper. "I don't suppose there's any point in leaving this with you."

Charly shrugged. "Go right ahead. Let me see if I have any matches on me. It would be fun to watch the last of him go up in smoke."

Trudy sighed again and moved away from the table. Charly stared at the folded newspaper. There wasn't one chance in a million she would read what Bret Roberts had to say.

She'd already disconnected her phone temporarily. Ever since Saturday, the man had been plaguing her with calls. She'd had to rip up several unopened telegrams, discard a postcard or two, refuse the delivery of flowers, and ask Trudy to cover for her on the store telephone; all callers were to be told she'd left town on an indefinite leave of absence.

When she mused about it, Charly only sank deeper into her blue funk. He'd been playing with her. How could he talk about honesty when during most of the time they'd spent together he hadn't told her who he was? He'd manipulated her into continuing to see him, assuaging all her fears, and then...

And then, even as she'd been working herself up to the height of nervous anxiety, ready at last to confide in the man she loved, he'd...well, he'd *known* already, exactly what it was that was worrying her to death. The very idea that he would now actually answer her confidential letter only added insult to injury. What on earth could the man possibly have to say at this point? "Dear Confidential, formerly Chicken Little, you were right, the sky is falling, sorry about that, sincerely, et cetera?" He had a lot of gall.

Charly moodily drummed her fingers on the table, staring at the upside-down column. She'd throw the damn thing out and be done with it. Charly picked the paper up gingerly, as if dead fish had been wrapped in the newsprint, and held it at arm's length. Out of the corner of her eye, she saw that Trudy was talking on the phone, her back to Charly. With a sudden growl of exasperation, she pulled the paper out flat, turned it right-side up, and started reading.

Mr. Heart wanted his readers to know that this column had been one of the great experiences of his life. Charly skimmed the opening paragraphs, practically snarling at the sincere gratitude so artfully expressed. She gathered that this column had been Bret's first try at journalism, and that he felt he'd been made to grow by the readers who took him seriously. Wasn't that nice?

She smiled in spite of herself at his wry recital of favorite whacko letters, then paused, frowning, at the next-to-last paragraph. He was reprimanding himself for the occasional times his advice had backfired, citing one recent instance that he especially regretted—giving advice to someone he knew personally.

If I thought I was being discreet, giving advice to her in print and keeping quiet when I saw her in person, I know now that this was wrong. An advice column is built on trust. You readers expect impartiality, and you deserve it. Yet the advice I gave my "friend" wasn't impartial, even though I thought I was acting in her best interest. I feel I must apologize publicly for any pain I have caused. Though other obligations would soon have forced me to retire from the column anyway, this incident has convinced me it's time to do so now. I'm reminded that Mr. Heart has an all-too-human heart of his own. So I guess it's time to say so long, and it's been good to know you. Hell, I've always distrusted authority figures, anyway.

Charly was surprised to feel a lump rising in her throat. She swallowed, frowning at the print in front of her, then read on.

Dear Confidential:

The condition you've written to me about is not at all uncommon, and is being treated more successfully all the time. In an earlier column, I listed three organizations in the Bay Area alone that will provide resources, and help you contact specialists in the field. But more importantly, you need to know that the problem you fear would "shatter" your future, is not a problem for the man who loves you.

Nothing on heaven or earth could change his feelings for you, his need to be with you and have you for his own. This man has a belief in your future together that is absolutely shatter-proof.

He loves you as you are, without reservation and with all his heart. He's yours for the asking. Just ask him!

Sincerely,
Mr. Heart

When Charly looked up from the paper, her eyes unaccountably blurring, she found Trudy standing by the table again.

"Well?" the older woman asked, looking at her watchfully.

"Well, what?" Charly replied. Pushing the newspaper away, she swallowed, blinked her eyes, and tried to maintain a front of composed cool as Trudy continued studying her.

"Well, what are you going to do now?"

"Nothing," Charly told her. "Look, so he's apologized. That was good of him. But it doesn't change the situation. Trudy, I didn't want to get involved with the man in the first place. I told you back then that I was happy on my own, and it's just as true now."

"You're not a very good liar," Trudy announced, shaking her head. "If you're happy, then I'm Harold's aunt."

Charly sighed, averting her eyes from Trudy's steady gaze. After nearly a week of feeling as though she'd suddenly been dropped into the bottom of a mine shaft, seeing Bret's words in print didn't immediately light up her world with happiness and joy.

"But what's the difference?" she said. "Bret wants children, I know he does. Even if we did get back together..." She shook her head. "But we won't. I don't want to chance it! I don't want to get turned all inside out and have my heart put through an emotional shredder again." She stopped, her throat choked up, the tears welling in her eyes. "I still say he acted like a... weasel. He says so, himself."

"All the more reason to respect him," Trudy countered promptly. "How many men do you know who would willingly own up to their mistakes like that?" She slapped her palm on the table with a vehemence that made Charly jump. "Charly, it's Mr. Heart! Remember? The man you said no man could measure up to? And he's not only sympathetic, strong, sensitive, and musculine—he's *cute!*" she exclaimed. "How could you turn a man like that down?"

"Easy," Charly snapped.

"It hasn't been easy for you, and you know it," Trudy argued. "You've been moping around here like a sick hound dog, as cranky as a shrew, and crying..." She paused as Charly blew her nose, then nodded. "I rest my case. Just look at you."

"Are you finished?" Charly asked.

"I suppose," Trudy grumbled. "The way I see it, you can forget about Bret Roberts, be uninvolved and miserable, or you can give him a second chance and have a chance at happiness, yourself. And that's my last word on the matter."

"Good," Charly said, wiping her eyes. The phone was ringing, and Trudy turned away with an archly imperious air, leaving Charly to contemplate her words and the sickly churning in the pit of her stomach.

She didn't want to admit that Trudy had a point. She knew in her heart that seeing Bret again couldn't make things any worse than they already were, and might even make them better. But some stubborn sense of pride was keeping her from him. Well, if he wanted her badly enough, he knew where to find her, didn't he? He'd probably be so wrapped up in his takeover of the *Voice* that his infatuation with her would fade. She knew about men's obsessions with their careers.

"Well, there goes another one," Trudy announced, a perplexed look on her face as she returned to the alcove.

"Another what?" Charly asked listlessly.

"Another animal to be delivered to the same address. Some Mr. Smith is either starting his own private zoo or an in-house pet shop." Trudy shrugged. "He's already bought himself a cat, a dog, a number of parakeets, a rabbit, a turtle—and now he wants Harold."

"Harold?" Charly sat up.

Trudy nodded. "It's the eighth animal he's ordered in five days. Started right after the weekend. *You* wouldn't know about such things, of course, seeing as you're off enjoying a leave of absence in Albania or some such place."

"If you want me to start answering the phones again," Charly said, with a twinge of guilt, "I guess I'm ready."

"That's more like it," Trudy said. "But actually, if you want to do something useful, why don't you take Harold over there? Robbie's got his hands full with that coral snake just now. It's within walking distance, over on Chestnut."

"The walk might get Harold out of his doldrums," Charly mused. "Besides, I wouldn't mind getting a look at this Mr. Smith. I'd like to make sure Harold's being put in good hands."

"Good idea," Trudy said. "I've never seen the fellow,

myself. The ordering's all been done by telephone—the man's secretary, I guess. We might want to determine that he's not some mad scientist trying to cross-breed a turtle with a parakeet," she added, chuckling.

Charly went to Harold's cage and found the chimp in his usual position—flat on his back, eyes gazing morosely into space. "Harold," Charly said, "you're about to get a new lease on life."

The chimp turned slightly, fixing her with a baleful, disinterested stare. Charly smiled. "Come on, sport," she said. "Fresh air, sunshine—that's what you need." Even as she said the words, she remembered who had said that very thing to her, not so long ago, in the greenery of Golden Gate Park, as he held her in his arms, azure eyes sparkling with mischief...

Charly sighed. She could use a new lease on life, herself.

It was warm enough now to wear just a linen jacket over a denim skirt and sleeveless halter. The sky was that remarkable color Charly had seen only here in San Francisco—a brilliant shiny blue untainted by urban pollution. She could feel spring in the warm breeze as she walked Harold up the hills toward his new residence-to-be.

But somehow she felt oddly removed from the beauty around her. Whereas a week ago, she would have drunk in every detail of budding greenery, savoring it with a lover's eye, she now felt deprived. That light-headed pleasure in the simplest things—that joy in the smile on a stranger's face or the sparkle of sun on a shop window—was no longer hers. It was gone as long as he was, she mused ruefully. Maybe it was gone for good.

Harold, on the other hand, had perked up considerably. He could barely keep hold of her hand, so excited was he to be out on the street again. Charly hoped that this mysterious patron, the man who was practically buying out their store in record time, had a spacious place, perhaps even a backyard. That would be great for Harold.

She turned the corner on Chestnut Street, keeping a firm grip on the chimp as the incline steepened. This was a prosperous-looking block, lined on both sides with Victorian houses in various pastel shades, their darker-hued trim highlighting each turn-of-the-century detail of cornice and curlicued gable. She checked the numbers as they ascended, noting that Mr. Smith's place was still higher on the hill.

By the time they reached it, Charly was a little winded. Harold's hairy hand in hers, she approached Mr. Smith's house, a picture perfect white and beige Victorian that had been lovingly preserved. She rang the doorbell.

"Yes?" The voice was muffled through the door.

"Hello, I'm delivering a chimpanzee to Mr. Smith, from The Sanctuary."

In a moment, the door swung open. Charly leaned forward, curious to see what sort of a man would be assembling a menagerie in this well-appointed house. She found herself looking at a blank space.

"Hi," said a voice.

Charly looked down. The door had been opened by a small boy with a baseball cap turned the wrong way on his head. He was beaming happily at the sight of Harold, only a foot shorter than he. Charly's heart skipped a beat and then beat faster.

"Smith!"

The boy looked up at her, his smile broadening. "Hey," he yelled over his shoulder, "it's her! She's here!"

Charly heard a clattering noise from inside, followed by a sneeze. She stiffened, pulse pounding.

"Come on in," Smith was saying, pulling at her skirt. "He's been waiting for you."

The second sneeze was louder and closer. Suddenly

Harold wasn't standing at her side, but bolting into the foyer, nearly knocking Smith over as he ran. And then Bret Roberts appeared, the chimp clinging to his legs, a sheepish smile on his face.

He was dressed with his usual lack of stylishness in a pair of worn corduroys and a short-sleeved sweat shirt, both smudged with paint. His hair was predictably uncombed, his feet bare . . . and his nose was a little red. But to Charly he looked exceedingly handsome. She found herself wondering, in a sort of daze, how she had managed to survive the last six days without those dazzling blue eyes gazing into hers, and those full, sensuous lips lighting up the air with a disarming grin.

"Charly," he said. "I thought you'd never get here."

Charly cleared her throat, trying to find her voice. "I . . . I hadn't planned on coming at all," she said.

Before she could protest, he'd reached out to take her hand and pull her inside. "Well, I'm going to make sure you don't run out again," he declared, gathering her into his arms.

Charly squirmed in his powerful grip, trying to push him away from her. Harold, hooting, sat down on the floor beside the wide-eyed, gaping Smith. "Bret," she fumed. "Let go! If you think you can solve anything by manhandling me . . ."

But in another moment it was too late. Bret's lips came down to claim hers with commanding force, silencing her protests with a kiss that wouldn't listen. His mouth met hers with urgent passion, parting her lips and rendering her breathless with the force of his need.

Charly felt herself surrendering, going limp as their kiss deepened. She felt her body mold its soft curves to his rangy frame.

The passion within her flamed, rising like a comet as his tongue sought hers. No longer passive, she answered his desire with her own pounding need, her tongue meeting his in a moist, swirling dance. The world disappeared and she knew only the delicious taste of him on her tongue, the scent and feel of him all around her. The ache she'd been carrying within her seemed suddenly to burst in grateful release.

Dimly she registered the sound of four hands applauding. Coming up for air, breaking her lips away from his and tearing her eyes from his smoldering blue ones, she looked down. Harold was clapping his hands over his head in a victorious salute, in imitation of the giggling Smith.

"Smith," Bret said, still holding Charly captive against him. "Why don't you take your friend here outside? Charly and I have some things to discuss."

"You're just going to kiss her again," said Smith, with thinly disguised distaste.

"Smith," Bret repeated. Sighing, the boy grabbed hold of Harold's hairy paw and began dragging him from the foyer.

"Bret . . ." Charly began.

"Charly . . ." he breathed, his lips closing over hers once more. For all of two seconds, Charly struggled to resist this encore of erotic arousal, then gave up, helpless, as the voluptuous feelings overcame her. She returned the kiss with a passion that matched his, reveling in the feel of his heart pounding against hers, his arms around her, hands fondling her soft curves.

When they finally broke apart, he stroked her cheek tenderly, a strangely sad expression in the depths of his glimmering eyes. "Charly," he whispered. "I didn't mean to hurt you."

"No?" she asked, trying to muster up her earlier ire. But it was impossible with him holding her this way.

"You read the paper today?" he asked. "I was hoping against hope that you'd—ah—" He turned away from her suddenly, face contorted in a violent sneeze.

"Bless you," she said. "Yes, I read the paper."

"Come with me," he said, taking her by the hand.

"Now, hold on, Bret," she began. "I didn't plan on coming to see you in the first place. How was I supposed to know you were the guy who was..."

She stopped, words trailing off in wonder as she entered the living room of the house. The place was a shambles. Pieces of furniture she recognized from Bret's houseboat and others less familiar were grouped haphazardly in the middle of the big room. One wall was painted a sparkling white, and the others were in the process of being plastered. Clearly he'd only begun moving in. But already, the room had become home for a mini-kingdom of animals.

There was The Sanctuary's Chinese dog, a little tabby cat she remembered, four birds in hanging cages, a familiar furry rabbit, and even a tankful of fish against one wall. Bret stood in the middle of the room, proudly extending his arms.

"Here, you see?" he said. "Just the sort of place you could feel at home in." He wrinkled his nose, covered it, and sneezed again.

"Bret, you're out of your mind," she said, unable to keep from smiling.

"Nope," he said solemnly. "I figured I could lure you in here if I kept buying pets—and I'm determined to enjoy living with them, dammit, even if it takes me a hundred allergy shots!"

"Bret," she said. "You didn't have to do this."

"After you refused all my calls, letters, telegrams? What else could I do?" He shrugged. "It's really only the cat that's a problem. But tell me, isn't this just the sort of place you'd like to live in? I got all your favorites."

He looked around him with a fiercely proprietary air, and Charly felt a surge of love for him and his ridiculous but well-meant ploy. She couldn't stop smiling as he sneezed again, the dog barked at a parakeet in one corner, and a turtle waddled slowly across the floor behind him.

"Bret, a houseful of pets won't solve everything," she said gently.

"It's a start, isn't it?" He met her bemused gaze. "Okay, so I got a little carried away." He moved back to take her hand in his. "But Charly, I'd do anything to make you happy."

Charly moved back, shivering involuntarily as his hand closed over hers. "I don't know why I'm even talking to you," she said. "After what you—"

"Charly, I'm sorry, you know I am. It started out as . . . as—" Again he fought back a sneeze, and gestured for her to come with him. Warily, she let him lead her from the room and out onto a sunlit verandah that overlooked a small backyard. Smith and Harold were chasing each other around the little lawn, both obviously delighted to have a new playmate.

"This is better," Bret murmured, guiding her to a white wicker loveseat. "First of all," he began, when he was seated beside her, "I think you should understand why I needed to conceal my identity as Mr. Heart to begin with."

"You mean, before you started playing your manipulative games with me?" she asked, unable to suppress an inner smile of satisfaction as Bret winced, shaking his head.

"Rub it in," he sighed. "You see, the Mr. Heart column was my first job on a newspaper, about seven years back. I had been on my own for a few years, without a penny of my father's to support me, and it was one of the only steady journalistic gigs I could find. Unfortunately, the *Sun* is one of Dad's papers. It was important to me that I get the job on the basis of my ability, not because of my last name, so I started the whole thing under this pen name."

"You mean, you were actually on your father's payroll and he didn't know it?"

Bret nodded. "Nobody at the *Sun* knew who Mr. Heart is, and I liked it that way. I really enjoyed the column. That's why I kept it up, even though I got much better jobs as time went by."

"And I suppose it wouldn't be the first thing you'd tell a woman," Charly said wryly. "But when you got Trudy's letter—"

"I know, I know." Bret shook his head. "I should have told you. But you seemed so damned set on giving me the gate, I just couldn't resist. It seemed harmless enough. I was only saying in the column what I'd be saying in person."

"And the second?"

Bret looked truly pained. "I never expected to get a second letter, Charly! I thought that first one would be the end of it," he said ruefully. "And by that time we were just starting to get to know each other. I was already head over heels in love, and I could tell you were running scared." He sighed. "I figured if I told you then, it would have made you distrust me."

"You would have been right," she said dryly. "And as it is—"

"Charly, listen to me," he said plaintively, taking her hand in his again. "I was about to tell you that day in Sausalito. As soon as I read the third letter I felt awful. I knew things had gone way too far. I was about to confess the whole wretched story and take the consequences when you found that stationery."

"I was so humiliated," she said quietly, staring at her hand in his.

"I'm sorry." His husky voice seemed to reflect heartfelt emotion. "I never thought things would get so out of hand. If I'd had any idea that your feelings were going to get hurt . . ." He shook his head.

There was a long silence between them. It seemed to Charly that she was listening to the pulse beating in her wrist, and the pulse of his thumb against hers, the rhythms finding a common beat.

"To tell you the truth, Charly," Bret said softly. "My feelings got a little scraped as well."

"Yours?" She looked up at him in surprise.

"Charly, when I told you I loved you, I meant it. And when I said I would marry you if I could, I meant that too. How do you think I felt when I found out you were keeping secrets because you didn't really trust my love?"

Charly stared at him, her throat tightening. "But I was too afraid to think anything else."

"Sweetheart," Bret said quietly, his hand squeezing hers with more force. "I guess you don't know me as well as I'd like you to. If you did, you'd know I wouldn't..." His voice trailed off, his features darkening. "What was he like, anyway—that guy who made your marriage so miserable? I think you should tell me now, Charly. I need to know why you mistrusted me so much from the start."

Charly exhaled a deep breath, looking away from Bret to the lawn below. "You're nothing like him," she said softly. "I realize that now. But it wasn't just Roy that tore up our marriage. It was my own selfishness, in a way." She bit her lower lip, then looked back at Bret. The sympathy she saw in his eyes gave her the courage to plunge on.

"I always wanted a child," she explained. "That's why, when I got pregnant after Roy and I had been going out for a year, I was really happy—even though we hadn't yet talked seriously about marriage." She smile ruefully. "And when Roy said he'd marry me, I was so excited that I didn't even sense he had misgivings. You see, he would rather have waited. He was just graduating that year, and he already had a good job lined up with a major computer firm. Marriage was okay, it fit in with his plans, but a child..." She shook her head. "He hadn't quite figured on that."

Charly stared at the green lawn, fighting down the lump in her throat, feeling the firm warmth of Bret's hand on hers. "I miscarried a few days after our honeymoon," she said simply, and sighed. "I felt so sad—and so angry—I couldn't even talk to anybody for a week. The doctors said I could try again, and Roy was with me. But still I was...devastated, I felt as if the world had ended, and he..." She looked away again. "I don't think he would have admitted it, even to himself, Bret, but I guess he was relieved."

Bret shook his head, his gaze still holding hers. Charly shrugged. "Well, his career was taking off. When I became obsessed with trying to have another child, he said it would be better to wait until he started making more money, until we could move to a bigger place. To tell you the truth, we were already growing a little distant. Roy was becoming more absorbed with his career, and I was totally wrapped up in my own needs. I wanted a baby so much..." Charly swallowed, cleared her throat.

"Go on," Bret said gently.

"Well, a miracle happened," Charly told him with a wry smile. "I did get pregnant again. And again I was so thrilled I couldn't see—or didn't want to see—that Roy was upset. I even thought a child would bring us closer again." She shook her head. "You see, when a woman's body betrays her like that, she can feel guilty. I thought the strains in our marriage were my fault for having lost the child. So now I was going to make up for it, and we'd be one happy family."

Charly sighed. "In fairness to Roy, I'll say that I was so caught up in my second pregnancy that I didn't pay much attention to him. But he got even in a pretty unfair way." She pursed her lips, staring into the space beyond

Bret. "He was convinced that I cared more about having a child than being his wife. Maybe he was right. Roy was the first man I'd slept with, and I didn't know very much about love. We weren't really kindred spirits to begin with, just two lustful college kids who had good times together. But somehow I guess I thought marriage would work out whatever differences there were between us . . ."

Charly looked back to meet Bret's gaze again. "Dumb, right? Well, Roy started having an affair with a woman at his office. I suppose she was giving him the attention he wanted. And you know what's funny? It didn't even seem to matter when I found out. Because by then I'd had my second miscarriage."

Bret swore softly beneath his breath. "Lord, Charly . . ."

"Yeah, *that* was a doozy," Charly said, shaking her head. "You never figure on the world ending twice— but it did," she said abruptly. "And I survived. And I divorced Roy." She was silent at last. The happy sounds of Harold and Smith at play seemed incongruous in the background.

Bret put both his hands around hers now. "I guess I can see why you've been so reluctant to jump into a new involvement," he said quietly.

Charly nodded, her throat tightening again. "It still scares me," she admitted. "And knowing that you *do* want children"—she gave him a pained smile—"makes it almost worse. How could you want me, knowing . . ."

"Charly." Bret's voice vibrated with a barely restrained fervor. "Don't you see? I love you for who you are, for the beauty I see in you, inside and out. I don't care what problems you have! I'd gladly take them on, darling. Anything you can throw at me: a troubled childhood, a fear of heights, a prison record, a wooden leg— hell, I'd live with it! What sort of a man do you think I am?"

His genuine indignation took her aback. For a moment Charly could only gaze at him in wonder. "But Bret, I know you want to settle down and have a family."

Bret grasped her by the shoulders. "Charly, I want *you*—first and most of all! Don't you understand how important you've become to me? Hell, you've turned my life upside down, thank goodness!"

He shook his head, loosening his grip on her. When he spoke again his voice was calmer, but his eyes had lost no luster as he held her questioning gaze. "Charly, from what you tell me, no doctor ever said you couldn't bear a child. There are dangers, sure—it is a risk. And I can understand your not wanting to take that risk. After all the trauma you've been through, no woman would be casual about trying again. But you *could* try—*if* you wanted to."

She stared at him, wanting to believe. And as she looked into his eyes, she felt a new hope rise inside her. The tremulous fears that would have dragged it down before were already evaporating under his warm and loving gaze.

"Of course I could try," she whispered, and smiled. "If you were with me."

"I'll be there for you, Charly, no matter what," he said firmly.

"There's no guaranteeing it would work, you know," she told him.

"I know," he said simply. "I'd be disappointed if it didn't, but I wouldn't love you any less, Charly. That's the truth."

Just as she felt her eyes fill, he drew her to him, hugging her close as the tears broke. He nestled her to his chest, his fingers stroking the soft skin of her neck and shoulder. Crooning her name, he rocked her gently and a flood of tears that seemed ages old was released at last in the shelter of his embrace.

She pressed against his strong body, knowing that

she'd finally found a sanctuary of her own. His soft kisses on her trembling eyelids soon stemmed the flow of tears. Tenderly, he wiped the last salty rivulets away, kissing her glistening cheeks with such careful thoroughness that at last she smiled.

"Charly," he murmured. "You've had it much too hard."

"It's certainly been hard this week," she admitted, sniffling. "I don't know if I could take things getting any harder—if I stayed away from you for good."

"You're not staying away, and I'm not going away," he said with a conviction that resounded through his chest against hers. "I want to spend the rest of my days making things a whole lot easier for you, Charly Lynn."

"Oh," she sighed. "That does sound good."

He cupped her chin with his hand, lifting her face so she could see the warmth and love shining in his bright blue eyes. "Well, then, listen to this: you can stop worrying about futures being shattered, okay? We're going to make our future up as we go along. Have you got that? Are you reading me loud and clear?"

Charly smiled, brushing her lips against the side of his hand as her whole being was flooded with a warm exultation. "I'm reading you, Bret."

"Good," he said, his eyes tender as he stroked her cheek. "Do you think you could learn to love a deceitful guy like me?"

"I'm afraid I've already learned," she sighed with mock-dismay. "I do love you, Bret."

"That's all I needed to hear." His lips brushed hers with exquisite gentleness. She returned the kiss with a more forceful passion, feeling that warmth grow in intensity as his tongue found hers and his arms enveloped her.

"Bret," she whispered. "If we do make it work, you and me . . ."

"Yes, love?"

"I think I would have the strength to try again. If you'd stand by me, I could try. I still want a child. Very badly . . ."

He hugged her to him even tighter. "It's all right, sweetheart. We can go one step at a time."

Again they kissed, more hungrily, drinking deeply of each other, entwined in the warmth of the sun and their mutual desire. She ran her fingers through his soft, thick hair, as his hands roved lovingly over the curves of her vibrant body.

"I just wanted you to know . . . I'm willing," she whispered.

"Willing?"

"Willing to try."

Bret smiled, kissing her chin and the sides of her pursed lips. "Well, that's something to look forward to," he said. "I can't think of a better way to spend our time . . ."

"Hmm?" She gazed at him as he stroked her hair.

"Well, sweetheart, I don't know if anyone's ever gone over this with you," he said, smiling slyly as his hands began roving from her shoulders to the softer curves below. "But this baby-making stuff doesn't really have anything to do with storks."

"No," she breathed, eyes widening.

"No," he whispered. "But it's got a lot to do with loving. And that's what's going to be occupying us from now on."

"Not running newspapers?" she teased. He shook his head. "Not putting this new apartment together?"

"Nope. You do like it, so far?"

She nodded. "Not getting all your allergy shots?"

For once he paused. "Allergy shots?"

Charly's eyes widened in mock-indignation. "My dear Mr. Heart," she said. "Didn't you say you'd do anything to make things up with me? Anything in the world?"

"That's right," Bret sighed. "Anything you want, my love."

She smiled, musing aloud: "It's a good thing that brass bed of yours has a nice, soft mattress."

Bret looked at her, eyes dark with desire as she lay back in his arms. "I've always liked it," he murmured. "Why?"

"Well, because you know where they give you those allergy shots, don't you?"

Bret's eyes widened as Charly's hand lightly traced the line of his buttocks. He cleared his throat. "Do I detect a certain gleeful anticipation in your voice? Maybe a little, ah, pointed revenge?"

Charly chuckled. "Perhaps a little."

"Darling," he said, "I think it's a small price to pay."

Second Chance at Love ®

___	0-425-08015-3	**PROMISE ME RAINBOWS #257** Joan Lancaster	$2.25
___	0-425-08016-1	**RITES OF PASSION #258** Jacqueline Topaz	$2.25
___	0-425-08017-X	**ONE IN A MILLION #259** Lee Williams	$2.25
___	0-425-08018-8	**HEART OF GOLD #260** Liz Grady	$2.25
___	0-425-08019-6	**AT LONG LAST LOVE #261** Carole Buck	$2.25
___	0-425-08150-8	**EYE OF THE BEHOLDER #262** Kay Robbins	$2.25
___	0-425-08151-6	**GENTLEMAN AT HEART #263** Elissa Curry	$2.25
___	0-425-08152-4	**BY LOVE POSSESSED #264** Linda Barlow	$2.25
___	0-425-08153-2	**WILDFIRE #265** Kelly Adams	$2.25
___	0-425-08154-0	**PASSION'S DANCE #266** Lauren Fox	$2.25
___	0-425-08155-9	**VENETIAN SUNRISE #267** Kate Nevins	$2.25
___	0-425-08199-0	**THE STEELE TRAP #268** Betsy Osborne	$2.25
___	0-425-08200-8	**LOVE PLAY #269** Carole Buck	$2.25
___	0-425-08201-6	**CAN'T SAY NO #270** Jeanne Grant	$2.25
___	0-425-08202-4	**A LITTLE NIGHT MUSIC #271** Lee Williams	$2.25
___	0-425-08203-2	**A BIT OF DARING #272** Mary Haskell	$2.25
___	0-425-08204-0	**THIEF OF HEARTS #273** Jan Mathews	$2.25
___	0-425-08284-9	**MASTER TOUCH #274** Jasmine Craig	$2.25
___	0-425-08285-7	**NIGHT OF A THOUSAND STARS #275** Petra Diamond	$2.25
___	0-425-08286-5	**UNDERCOVER KISSES #276** Laine Allen	$2.25
___	0-425-08287-3	**MAN TROUBLE #277** Elizabeth Henry	$2.25
___	0-425-08288-1	**SUDDENLY THAT SUMMER #278** Jennifer Rose	$2.25
___	0-425-08289-X	**SWEET ENCHANTMENT #279** Diana Mars	$2.25
___	0-425-08461-2	**SUCH ROUGH SPLENDOR #280** Cinda Richards	$2.25
___	0-425-08462-0	**WINDFLAME #281** Sarah Crewe	$2.25
___	0-425-08463-9	**STORM AND STARLIGHT #282** Lauren Fox	$2.25
___	0-425-08464-7	**HEART OF THE HUNTER #283** Liz Grady	$2.25
___	0-425-08465-5	**LUCKY'S WOMAN #284** Delaney Devers	$2.25
___	0-425-08466-3	**PORTRAIT OF A LADY #285** Elizabeth N. Kary	$2.25
___	0-425-08508-2	**ANYTHING GOES #286** Diana Morgan	$2.25
___	0-425-08509-0	**SOPHISTICATED LADY #287** Elissa Curry	$2.25
___	0-425-08510-4	**THE PHOENIX HEART #288** Betsy Osborne	$2.25
___	0-425-08511-2	**FALLEN ANGEL #289** Carole Buck	$2.25
___	0-425-08512-0	**THE SWEETHEART TRUST #290** Hilary Cole	$2.25
___	0-425-08513-9	**DEAR HEART #291** Lee Williams	$2.25

Prices may be slightly higher in Canada.

Available at your local bookstore or return this form to:

SECOND CHANCE AT LOVE
Book Mailing Service
P.O. Box 690, Rockville Centre, NY 11571

Please send me the titles checked above. I enclose _____. Include 75¢ for postage and handling if one book is ordered; 25¢ per book for two or more not to exceed $1.75. California, Illinois, New York and Tennessee residents please add sales tax.

NAME _____

ADDRESS _____

CITY _____ STATE/ZIP _____

(allow six weeks for delivery)   SK-41b

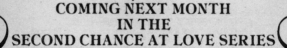

COMING NEXT MONTH
IN THE
SECOND CHANCE AT LOVE SERIES

QUESTIONNAIRE

1. How do you rate _____
   (please print TITLE)
   - ☐ excellent   ☐ good
   - ☐ very good   ☐ fair   ☐ poor

2. How likely are you to purchase another book in this series?
   - ☐ definitely would purchase
   - ☐ probably would purchase
   - ☐ probably would not purchase
   - ☐ definitely would not purchase

3. How likely are you to purchase another book by this author?
   - ☐ definitely would purchase
   - ☐ probably would purchase
   - ☐ probably would not purchase
   - ☐ definitely would not purchase

4. How does this book compare to books in other contemporary romance lines?
   - ☐ much better
   - ☐ better
   - ☐ about the same
   - ☐ not as good
   - ☐ definitely not as good

5. Why did you buy this book? (Check as many as apply)
   - ☐ I have read other
     SECOND CHANCE AT LOVE romances
   - ☐ friend's recommendation
   - ☐ bookseller's recommendation
   - ☐ art on the front cover
   - ☐ description of the plot on the back cover
   - ☐ book review I read
   - ☐ other _____
     _____
     _____

(Continued...)

6. Please list your three favorite contemporary romance lines.

_____
_____
_____

7. Please list your favorite authors of contemporary romance lines.

_____
_____
_____
_____
_____
_____

8. How many SECOND CHANCE AT LOVE romances have you read? _____

9. How many series romances like SECOND CHANCE AT LOVE do you <u>read</u> each month? _____

10. How many series romances like SECOND CHANCE AT LOVE do you <u>buy</u> each month? _____

11. Mind telling your age?
    ☐ under 18
    ☐ 18 to 30
    ☐ 31 to 45
    ☐ over 45

☐ Please check if you'd like to receive our <u>free</u> SECOND CHANCE AT LOVE Newsletter.

We hope you'll share your other ideas about romances with us on an additional sheet and attach it securely to this questionnaire.

• •

Fill in your name and address below:
Name _____
Street Address _____
City _____ State _____ Zip _____

Please return this questionnaire to:
    SECOND CHANCE AT LOVE
    The Berkley Publishing Group
    200 Madison Avenue, New York, New York 10016